Seven Icelandic Short Stories

Reykjavik
The Ministry Of Education

by

Ed. Ásgeir Pétursson And
Steingrímur J. Þorsteinsson

Double9 BOOKS

Seven Icelandic Short Stories

Reykjavik
The Ministry Of Education

by Ed. Ásgeir Pétursson And
Steingrímur J. Þorsteinsson

ISBN: 978-93-76394-09-8

Published by

DOUBLE 9 BOOKS
2/13-B, Ansari Road
Daryaganj, New Delhi – 110002
info@double9books.com
www.double9books.com
Tel. 011-40042856

ABOUT THE AUTHOR

Asgeir Petursson and Steingrimur J Thorsteinsson are associated with the preservation and presentation of Icelandic literary tradition, and their names are often connected with editorial work that highlights the importance of national storytelling, their roles can be understood through the broader significance of Icelandic editors who dedicate their efforts to safeguarding written heritage. Such figures typically focus on selecting, organizing, and contextualizing texts that reflect the values, challenges, and imaginative depth of a culture shaped by its landscape and history. Their contributions often involve bringing attention to stories that capture moral reflection, human resilience, and the connection between individuals and their environment. By engaging in editorial work, they support the continuation of a literary tradition rooted in clarity of language and respect for narrative craft. Through their involvement, they contribute to ensuring that significant stories remain accessible, allowing readers to appreciate the richness of Icelandic thought, the endurance of its cultural identity, and the importance of preserving narratives that speak to both community and individuality.

CONTENTS

INTRODUCTION

I

Of the seven Icelandic short stories which appear here, the first was probably written early in the thirteenth century, while the rest all date from the early twentieth century. It might therefore be supposed that the earliest of these stories was written in a language more or less unintelligible to modern Icelanders, and that there was a gap of many centuries in the literary production of the nation. This, however, is not the case.

The Norsemen who colonized Iceland in the last quarter of the ninth century brought with than the language then spoken throughout the whole of Scandinavia. This ancestor of the modern Scandinavian tongues has been preserved in Iceland so little changed that every Icelander still understands, without the aid of explanatory commentaries, the oldest preserved prose written in their country 850 years ago. The principal reasons for this were probably limited communications between Iceland and other countries, frequent migrations inside the island, and, not least important, a long and uninterrupted literary tradition. As a consequence, Icelandic has not developed any dialects in the ordinary sense.

It is to their language and literature, as well as to the island separateness of their country, that the 175 thousand inhabitants of this North-Atlantic state of a little more than a hundred thousand square kilometres owe their existence as an independent and separate nation.

The Icelanders established a democratic legislative assembly, the Althingi (Alþingi) in 930 A.D., and in the year 1000 embraced Christianity. Hence there soon arose the necessity of writing down the law and translations of sacred works. Such matter, along with historical knowledge, may well have constituted the earliest writings in Icelandic, probably dating as far back as the eleventh century, while the oldest preserved texts were composed early in the twelfth century. This was the beginning of the so-called saga- writing. The important thing was that most of what was written down was in the vernacular, Latin being used but sparingly. Thus a literary style was evolved which soon reached a high standard. This style, so forceful in its perspicuity, was effectively simple, yet rich in the variety of its classical structure.

There were different categories of sagas. Among the most important were the sagas of the Norwegian kings and the family sagas. The latter tell us about the first generations of native Icelanders. They are all anonymous and the majority of them were written in the thirteenth century. Most of them contain a more or less historical core. Above all, however, they are fine literature, at times realistic, whose excellence is clearly seen in their descriptions of events and character, their dialogue and structure. Most of them are in fact in the nature of historical novels. The Viking view of life pervading them is characteristically heroic, but with frequent traces of the influence of Christian writing.

Besides these there were short stories (þaettir) about Icelanders, of which THE STORY OF AUDUNN AND THE BEAR (Auðunar þáttr vestfirzka) is one of the best known. [Footnote: In this edition, the specially-Icelandic consonants þ and ð are printed as th and d respectively, and the superstressed vowels á,í,ó, and ú, are given without the acute accent, when they occur in proper names in the stories, e. g. Þórður: Thordur.]

These may be regarded as a preliminary stage in the development of the longer family saga, simpler, yet having essentially the same characteristics. Both types then continued to be written side by side. Although the geographical isolation of the country was stated above as one of the reasons for the preservation of the language, too great a stress should not be laid on this factor, especially not during the early centuries of the settlement. The Icelanders were great and active navigators who discovered Greenland (shortly after 980) and North America (Leifr Eiriksson, about 1000). Thus THE STORY OF AUDUNN AND THE BEAR recounts travels to Greenland, Norway, Denmark and Italy. It was then fashionable for young Icelanders to go abroad and spend some time at the courts of the Norwegian kings, where the skalds recited poems of praise dedicated to the king. In this story the occasion of the voyage is a less common one, the bringing of a polar bear as a gift to the Danish king. In several other Icelandic stories, and in some of other countries, we read of such gifts, and of how European potentates prized these rare creatures from Greenland.

In Scandinavia, Germany, and elsewhere, there have been legends similar to the story of Audunn, where a man, after having been to the Norwegian king with a tame bear, decides to present it to the king of Denmark. However, we know of no earlier source for this motif than the story of Audunn. Whatever its value as historical fact, it could well be the model to which the other versions might be traced. This story is preserved in the Morkinskinna, an Icelandic manuscript written in the second half of the thirteenth century, as well as in several later manuscripts. [Footnote: The most valuable edition of THE STORY OF ADUNN AND THE BEAR is that of Guðni Jónsson in the series Íslenzk fornrit (vol. VI. Reykjavík 1943).

The text of this edition is followed in the present translation, except in a few cases where reference has been made to the texts of Fornmannasögur VI, Copenhagen 1831, and Flateyjarbók III, Oslo 1868.] The story had probably been written down by 1220, if not earlier. It is given a historical background in so far as it is set in the time of Haraldr the Hard-ruler, King of Norway (1046-66), and Sveinn Úlfsson, King of Denmark (1047-76), when the two countries were at war (c. 1062- 64). Both monarchs are depicted as generous, magnanimous men, but Audunn was shrewd enough to see which would give the greater reward for his precious bear. For all his generosity, King Haraldr was known to be ruthless and grasping. What the writer had in mind may have been a character-comparison of the two kings and the description of "one of the luckiest of men", about whom the translator, G. Turville-Petre says: "Audunn himself, in spite of his shrewd and purposeful character, is shown as a pious man, thoughtful of salvation, and richly endowed with human qualities, affection for his patron and especially for his mother. The story is an optimistic one, suggesting that good luck may attend those who have good morals."

II

The Icelanders have never waged war against any nation. But in the thirteenth century they were engaged in a civil war which ended in their submitting to the authority of the Norwegian king in the sixties (this authority was transferred to the King of the Danes in 1380). It is interesting that, during the next few decades after this capitulation, saga-writing seems to reach a climax as an art, in family sagas like Njáls saga, "one of the great prose works of the world" (W. P. Ker). It is as if the dangers of civil war and the experiences gained in times of surrender had created in the authors a kind of inner tension—as if their maturity had found full expression in the security of peace. However, with the first generation born in Iceland in subjection, the decline of saga- writing seems to begin. This can hardly be a mere coincidence. On the contrary it was brought about by a number of different factors.

Subsequently, in the fourteenth century, saga-writing becomes for the most part extinct. From c. 1400-1800 there is hardly any prose fiction at all. Hence the fact that several centuries remain unrepresented in this work (though the gap might have been reduced to four or five centuries had literary-historical considerations alone been allowed to influence the present selection).

But the sagas continued to be copied and read. After the setting up of the first printing press (c. 1530), and after the Reformation (c. 1550), religious literature grew much in bulk, both translations (that of the Bible was printed in 1584) and original works, and a new kind of historical writing came into being. Side by side with scholars, we have self-educated commoners who wrote both prose and, especially, poetry.

In Iceland, being a "poet" has never been considered out of the ordinary. On the contrary, a person unable to make up a verse or two would almost be considered exceptional. Yet, this requires considerable skill as the Icelanders are the only nation that has preserved the ancient common Germanic alliteration (found in all Germanic poetry till late medieval times). We frequently find this device accompanied by highly complicated rhyme schemes. Despite this rather rigid form, restrictive perhaps, yet disciplinary in its effect, exquisite poetry has nevertheless been produced. This poetry, however, is not within the scope of this introduction. Suffice it to say that from what exists of their verse it is clear that poets have been active at all times since the colonization of the country. It is this uninterrupted flow of poetry that above all has helped to preserve the language and the continuity of the literary tradition.

During the centuries we have been discussing—especially, however, the seventeenth—the Icelanders probably wrote more verse than any other nation has ever done—ranging in quality, to be sure, from the lowest to the highest. When, in the sixteenth century, they had got paper to take the place of the more expensive parchment, they could universally indulge in copying old literature and writing new, an opportunity which they certainly made use of. It was their only luxury—and, at the same time, a vital need.

We have said that the Icelanders had never waged war against any other people. But they have had to struggle against foreign rulers, and against hardships caused by the nature of their country. After the Reformation, the intervention of the Crown greatly increased, and, at the same time, its revenues from the country. A Crown monopoly of all trade was imposed (in 1602). Nature joined forces with mismanagement by the authorities; on the seas surrounding the island pack-ice frequently became a menace to shipping, and there also occurred unusually long and vicious series of volcanic eruptions. These culminated in the late eighteenth century (1783), when the world's most extensive lava fields of historical times were formed, and the mist from the eruption was carried all over Europe and far into the continent of Asia. Directly or indirectly as a consequence of this eruption, the greater part of the live-stock, and a fifth of the human population of the country perished.

Still the people continued to tell stories and to compose poems. No doubt the Icelanders have thus wasted on poetical fantasies and visionary daydreams much of the energy that they might otherwise have used in life's real battle. But the greyness of commonplace existence became more bearable when they listened to tales of the heroic deeds of the past. In the evening, the living-room (baðstofa), built of turf and stone, became a little more cheerful, and hunger was forgotten, while a member of the household read, or sang, about far-away knights and heroes, and the banquets they gave in splendid halls. In their imagination people thus tended to make their environment seem larger, and better, than life, as did Hrolfur with his fishing-boat in the story When I was on the Frigate.

III

About 1800, things began to improve. The monopoly of trade, which had been relaxed in 1787, was finally abolished in 1854. In the year 1874 Iceland got self-government in its internal affairs, and in 1904 its first minister of state with residence in the country. It became a sovereign kingdom in union with Denmark in 1918, and an independent republic in 1944.

The climate of the country has improved during the last hundred and fifty years, though there were a number of severe years in the eighteen eighties. It was at this time that emigration to the North- American Continent reached a peak, especially to Canada, where one of the settlements came to be called New Iceland—the title given to the last story in this book. Many of these emigrants suffered great hardships, and, as the story tells, several of them became disillusioned with the land of promise. Their descendants, however, have on the whole done well in the New World.

Until recently, the Icelanders were almost entirely a nation of farmers, and the majority of the stories in this collection contain sketches of country life. A certain amount of perseverance and even obstinacy was needed for a farmer's life on an island skirting the Arctic Circle (The Old Hay). Only about a quarter of the country is fit for human habitation, mainly the districts along the coast. The uplands, for the most part made up of mountains, glaciers, sand- deserts, and lava, are often awe-inspiring in their grandeur.

Nevertheless it would be wrong to exaggerate the severity of the land. In many places the soil is fertile, as is often the case in volcanic countries, and—thanks to the Gulf Stream, which flows up to the shores of the island—the climate is a good deal more temperate than one might suppose (the average annual temperatures in Reykjavík are 4-5° Centigrade).

Besides, the surrounding sea makes up for the barrenness of the country by having some of the richest fishing banks in the world. Hence, in addition to being farmers, the Icelanders have always been fishermen who brought means of sustenance from the sea—usually in primitive open boats like those described in When I was on the Frigate and Father and Son. In the late nineteenth century decked vessels came into use besides the open boats, succeeded by steam trawlers at the beginning of the present century.

For the last few decades, the Icelanders have been employing a modern fishing fleet, and, at the time of writing, fishery products constitute more than ninety per cent of the country's exports.

With the growth of the fisheries and commerce there began to spring up towards the end of the nineteenth century a number of trading villages in different parts of the country. Reykjavík, the only municipality of fairly long standing and by far the biggest one, had at the turn of the present century a population of only between six and seven thousand—now about eleven times that number. We catch glimpses of these small trading stations at the beginning of the twentieth century in A Dry Spell and Father and Son.

Nowadays, four fifths of the population live in villages and townships—where some light industry has sprung up—and, in Reykjavík alone, more than two fifths of the population are concentrated.

In the last fifty years, the occupations of the people and their culture have changed from being in many respects medieval, and have assumed modern forms. The earlier turfbuilt farmhouses have now been replaced by comfortable concrete buildings which get their electricity from a source of water power virtually inexhaustible. Many of these,—e. g. the majority of houses in Reykjavík—are heated by water from hot springs, so that the purity of the northern air is seldom spoilt by smoke from coal-fires. The reliable Icelandic pony—so dear to the farmer in New Iceland, and for long known as "a man's best friend"—has now for the most part come to serve the well-to-do who can afford to use it for their joy-rides, its place in farmwork being taken by modern agricultural machinery. As a means of travel it has been replaced by a host of motorcars, and by aeroplanes, which in Iceland are as commonly used in going from one part of the country to another as railway trains in other countries. In fact, it has not been found feasible to build railways in Iceland. Besides this, a large number of airliners make daily use of Icelandic airfields on transatlantic flights. What with most other nations has been a slow and gradual process lasting several centuries, has in Iceland come about in more or less a revolutionary way. It is therefore not to be wondered at that there should have been a certain instability in the development of the urban and economic life of the country. In this field, however, there appear to be signs of consolidation.

Foreigners who come to this country in search of the old saga-island are sometimes a little disappointed at finding here, in place of saga-tellers and bards, a modern community, with its own university, a national theatre, and a symphony orchestra. Be this as it may, literature still holds first place among the arts and cultures. A collection of books is indeed considered as essential a part of a home as the furniture itself. For such visitors, there may be some consolation in the fact that in some places they may have quite a job in spotting the grocer's among the bookshops.

IV

In literature there had, especially in poetry, been a continuity from the very beginnings. Yet, in the field also, the early nineteenth century saw the dawn of a new age. The Romantic Movement was here, as elsewhere, accompanied by a national awakening, so that literature became the herald and the principal motive force of social improvement. There was at the same time a new drive for an increased beauty of language and refinement of style, where the classical, cultivated, literary language and the living speech of the time merged. With Romanticism there also emerged poets of so great merit that only a few such had come forward since the end of the saga period. But henceforward—let's take as our point of departure the second quarter of the nineteenth century—each generation in the country has indeed produced some outstanding literary works, comparable in quality with the accomplishments of the ancient classical Edda and saga periods.

During this new golden age, several literary tendencies and genres may be observed. But Romanticism remained the most lasting and potent literary force for about a century. However, one of the characteristics of the Icelandic literature of later ages is the infrequent manifestation of literary trends in their purest and most extreme forms. Here the stabilizing and moderating influence of the ancient sagas has, without doubt, been at work. In most cases this middle course may be said to have been beneficial to the literature.

But the saga-literature may also well have had a restraining influence on later authors in so far as it set a difficult standard to be emulated. It is probably here that the principal explanation of the late re-emergence of prose fiction is to be sought. It was not until about the middle of the nineteenth century that modern short stories, novels and plays began to be written on anything like a scale worthy of note. The earliest of these were romantic in spirit, though most of them had a realistic tinge. With Realism, the short story came into its own in the eighties and nineties of the last century. This trend came like a fresh current to take its place side by side with Romanticism, without, however, ousting it from the literary scene. But owing to the realistic technique and the tragic endings of much in the ancient literature—Eddaic poetry and sagas alike—Realism was never the novel force it generally was felt to be elsewhere. Still, it brought social criticism into our literature. This was introduced through the activity of young literary-minded students who, while studying at the University of Copenhagen, had become full of enthusiasm for Georg Brandes and his school.

One of these young men was Einar H. Kvaran (1859-1938), a clergyman's son from the North, who, after beginning as a student of politics, soon turned his attention to literature and journalism. He became editor of Icelandic newspapers in Canada (1885-95), and, later, in Iceland, mainly in Reykjavík. His chief preoccupation, however, became the composition of short stories and novels, and besides these he also wrote some plays and poetry. The delicacy and the religious bent of his nature could not for long remain the soil for the satirical asperity and materialism of the realist school, though his art was always marked by its technique. As he advanced in years, brotherhood and forgiveness became an evergrowing element in his idealism, and he became the first bearer of the spiritualist message in this country. With his stories he had a humanizing influence on his times, especially in the education of children, and in the field of culture he remained actively interested right up to a ripe old age. If somewhat lacking in creative fervour and colourful raciness of style, he made up for it by the abundance of his intelligence, his humanity and culture.

He wrote A Dry Spell (Ðurrkur) at the beginning of the present century, when he had disengaged himself from the strongest influence of Realism, but before moral preaching and the belief in the life hereafter had become the leading elements in his stories. He had then, for a few years, been living in the north-country town of Akureyri, which obviously provides the model for the setting of the story. It was first printed in the 1905 issue of the periodical Skírnir.

In addition to the travelled, academic realists, there appeared a group of self-educated popular writers, some of whom had come into direct contact with this foreign school. They were farmers, even in the more remote country districts, who had read the latest Scandinavian literature in the original, and who wrote stories containing radical social satire. Guðmundur Friðjónsson, for instance, had begun his career in this way. In many of these authors, however, we find rather a sort of native realism, where there is not necessarily a question of the influence of any particular literary tendency. Their works sprang out of the native environment of the authors, whose vision, despite a limited horizon, was often vivid. They convey true impressions of real life.

Of this kind are most of the works of Guðmundur Friðjónsson (1869-1944), a radical who later turned to conservatism—and the best works of Jón Trausti (1873-1918). These, who had their debut as writers about the turn of the century, are the authors of the next two stories in our collection. Both were North-countrymen. The former, a farmer's son from a district enjoying a high standard of culture, himself settled down as a farmer in his native locality in order to earn a living for his large family. In his youth he had attended a secondary school in the neighbourhood for a couple of winters, but he never had his experiences enriched by foreign travel and was during the whole of his life anchored to his native region. Jón Trausti, the son of a farm labourer and his wife, who had been born on one of the northernmost farms in Iceland in a barren and outlying district, was brought up in dire poverty. From an early age he had had to fend for himself as a farmhand and fisherman, finally settling in Reykjavík as a printer. Apart from his apprenticeship with the printers, he never went to any sort of school (school education was first made compulsory by law in Iceland in 1907); but on two occasions he had travelled abroad.

These energetic persons became widely read, especially in Icelandic literature, and wrote extensively under difficult circumstances:—in fact all the modern authors represented in the present book may be said to have been prolific as writers. Guðmundur Friðjónsson was equally versatile as a writer of short stories and poems. He has a rich command of imagery and diction, and his style, at times a little pompous, is often powerful though slightly archaic in flavour. The ancient heroic literature doubtless fostered his manly ideas, which, however, sprang from his own experience in life. One must, he felt, be hard on oneself, and on one's guard against the vanity of newfangled ideas and against the enervating effect of civilization. It is in the nature of things that with this farmer and father of a family of twelve, assiduity, prudence, and self- discipline should be among the highest virtues. This is notably apparent in The Old Hay (Gamla heyið), which he wrote in 1909, and which was published in Tólf sögur (Twelve stories) in 1915.

Jón Trausti (pseudonym of Guðmundur Magnússon) is best known as the author of novels and short stories on contemporary and historical themes, but he also wrote plays and poems. He was endowed with fertile creative powers and the ability to draw vivid sketches of environment and character. At times, however, he lacks restraint, especially in his longer novels. Still, his principal work, The Mountain Cot (Heiðarbýlið)—one of the longest cycles in Icelandic fiction—is his greatest. The little outlying mountain cot becomes a separate world in its own right, a coign of vantage affording a clear view of the surrounding countryside where we get profound insight into human nature. Like the bulk of his best work, this novel has a foundation in his own experiences. In reading the story by him included in this volume, the reader may find it helpful to bear in mind Trausti's early life as a fisherman. What he attempts to show us there is a kind of inner reality—an offset to reality. When I was on the Frigate (Þegar eg var á fregátunni) first published in Skírnir for 1910.

Jón Trausti and Einar H. Kvaran—who between them form an interesting contrast—were the most prolific novelists at the beginning of the present century. By that time prose was becoming an increasingly important part of Icelandic literature. It would be more or less true to say that in the first thirty years of the century it had gained an equal footing with poetry. For the last thirty years, however, prose has taken first place, after poetry had constituted the backbone of Icelandic literature for six hundred years, or since the end of saga-writing.

But there were several writers who felt that the small reading public at home in Iceland gave them too little scope. So they emigrated, mostly to Denmark, and in the early decades of the century began to write in foreign languages, though the majority continued simultaneously to write in the vernacular. Pioneers in this field were the dramatist Johann Sigurjónsson (1880-1919), and the novelist Gunnar Gunnarsson (b. 1889). Both of these wrote in Danish as well as in Icelandic. Early in the second decade of the century three of this overseas group produced works that were accorded immediate acclaim, and which have since become classics, being widely translated into foreign languages. These were Eyvind of the Hills (Fjalla-Eyvindur) by Johann Sigurjonsson; The Borg Family (Borgaraettin, in English Guest the One-eyed) by Gunnar Gunnarsson; and Nonni, Erlebnisse eines jungen Isländers, the first of the famous children's books by the Jesuit monk Jón Sveinsson (Jon Svensson, 1857-1944). With these works modern Icelandic literature won for the first time a place for itself among the living contemporary literatures of the world. Since then, Iceland's contribution has been steady, not only in the works of those who wrote in foreign languages, but equally—and during the last couple of decades exclusively—in vernacular writing. In fact, with the return to his native country of Gunnar Gunnarsson in 1939, the vogue of writing in foreign languages virtually came to an end.

On his arrival in Iceland Gunnarsson had settled in his native east-country district though he afterwards moved to Reykjavík, where he now lives. Indeed he possesses many of the best qualities of the gentleman-farmer—firmness, tenacity of purpose, and a craving for freedom in his domain,—combined with a writer's imaginative and narrative powers and understanding of humanity. He often describes human determination and man's struggle with destiny, especially in his historical novels, which are set in most periods of Icelandic history. More moving, perhaps, are his novels on contemporary themes. The greatest among these is the cycle The Church on the Mountain (Fjallkirkjan; of the five novels making up this sequence, three have been translated into English under two titles, Ships in the Sky and The Night and the Dream). This is one of the major works of Icelandic literature—containing a fascinating world of fancy, invention, and reality.

It is the story of the development of a writer who leaves home in order to seek the world. One of the best known stories in all Icelandic literature is his masterly short novel Advent or The good Shepherd (Aðventa).—Father and Sam Feðgarnir) was first published in the periodical Eimreiðin in 1916. The present version, with slight changes, is that found in the author's collected works, Rit XI, 1951.

Most Icelandic writers have, of course, written in the vernacular only, in spite of longer or shorter stay abroad. This applies to the last two authors represented here, both of whom appeared on the literary scene about 1920.

Guðmundur G. Hagalín (b. 1898) comes from the sea-girt Western Fiords, where he was a fisherman before attending secondary school. Later, he lectured on Iceland in Norway for a few years (1924-27), and is now a superintendent of public libraries. His home is in the neighbourhood of Reykjavík. In his novels, and more particularly in his short stories, he is at his best in his portrayals of the simple sturdy seamen and countryfolk of his native region, which are often refreshingly arch in manner. Hagalín, who is a talented narrator, frequently succeeds in catching the living speech and characteristic mode of expression of his characters. The Fox Skin (Tófuskinnið) first appeared in 1923, in one of his collections of short stories (Strandbúar).—He has also been successful as a recorder and editor of the biographies of greatly different people, based on first-hand accounts of their own lives. He is at present continuing with the writing of his autobiography—a long and interesting work.

Halldór Kiljan Laxness was born in 1902 in Reykjavík. Shortly afterwards his parents established themselves on a farm in the neighbourhood where he was brought up, and where he has now built himself a home. He is a patriot and, at the same time, a cosmopolitan who has probably travelled more extensively abroad than any other of his fellow-countrymen. After becoming a Catholic at the age of twenty, he spent a year in monasteries abroad, but had already begun to waver in his Catholicism when he first visited America, where he stayed from 1927 to 1930. During those years he became more and more radical in his social beliefs. Already in his first year there, he wrote the short story New Iceland (Nýja Ísland), which was immediately published in Heimskringla, an Icelandic weekly in Winnipeg. The story thus dates from an early period, when his art was in process of great development.

Indeed, the nineteen twenties saw important changes in our literature. The last of the great nineteenth century poets were vanishing from the literary scene, their places being taken by others, whose poetry, though hardly as profound and lofty in conception, was more lyrical and simple in manner, with greater delicacy and refinement of form. Especially in the prose-writing of the period, there were signs of flourishing growth.

Gunnar Gunnarsson wrote The Church on the Mountain, and Laxness was becoming known. In the early thirties he appears as a fully mature writer in Salka Valka, a political love story from a fishing village, and Independent People (Sjálfstaett fólk), a heroic novel about the stubbornness and the lot of the Icelandic mountain farmer, both of which have appeared in English translations. Laxness has devoted less attention to the writing of plays and poetry than novels and short stories. Two among his greatest works are the novel sequences The Light of the World (Heimsljós)—about a poet-genius who never reaches maturity—, and The Bell of Iceland (Íslandsklukkan), a historical novel describing a political, cultural and human struggle. On the whole, the subject-matter of his stories is extremely varied, equally as regards time, place and human types. However, the greatest variety will probably be found in his style, which he constantly adapts to suit the subject. Behind all this lies a fertile creativeness which rarely leaves the reader untouched. No matter where in the wide world his stories may be set, they always stand in some relation to his people—though, at the same time, he usually succeeds in endowing them with universal values shared by common humanity. To achieve this has from early on been Laxness' aim; thus the first printed version of New Iceland contains the sub-heading: "An international proletarian story."

When this introduction was being written, a new novel by him, Heaven Reclaimed (Paradísarheimt) was published (1960), which, like his early short story, is set partly in America—this time among the Icelandic Mormons of Utah. Here, the man who goes out across half the world in quest of the millennium is in the end led back to his origins.

Laxness was awarded the Nobel Prize in 1955.

Tke University of Iceland, Reykjavík.

Steingrímur J. Þorsteinsson.

ANONYMOUS

THE STORY OF AUDUNN AND THE BEAR

EARLY 13TH CENTURY

I

There was a man called Audunn; he came of a family of the Western Firths, and was not well off. Audunn left Iceland from the Western Firths with the assistance of Thorsteinn, a substantial farmer, and of Thorir, a ship's captain, who had stayed with Thorsteinn during the winter. Audunn had been on the same farm, working for Thorir, and as his reward he got his passage to Norway under Thorir's care.

Audunn had set aside the greater part of his property, such as it was, for his mother, before he took ship, and it was determined that this should support her for three years.

Now they sailed to Norway and had a prosperous voyage, and Audunn spent the following winter with the skipper Thorir, who had a farm in Moérr. The summer after that, they sailed out to Greenland, where they stayed for the winter.

It is told that in Greenland, Audunn bought a white bear, a magnificent beast, and paid for him all he had. Next summer they returned to Norway, and their voyage was without mishap. Audunn brought his bear with him, intending to go south to Denmark to visit King Sveinn, and to present the beast to him. When he reached die south of Norway and came to the place where the King was in residence, Audunn went ashore, leading his bear, and hired lodgings.

King Haraldr was soon told that a bear had been brought to the place, a magnificent creature, belonging to an Icelander. The King immediately sent men to fetch Audunn, and when he entered the King's presence, Audunn saluted him as was proper. The King acknowledged the salute suitably and then asked:

Is it true that you have a great treasure, a white bear?

Audunn answered and said that he had got a bear of some sort.

The King said: Will you sell him to us for the price you paid for him?

Audunn answered: I would not care to do that, my Lord.

Will you then, said the King, have me pay twice the price? That would be fairer if you gave all you had for him.

I would not care to do that, my Lord, answered Audunn, but the King said:

Will you give him to me then?

No, my Lord, answered Audunn.

The King asked: What do you mean to do with him then?—and Audunn answered: I mean to go south to Denmark and give him to King Sveinn.

Can it be that you are such a fool, said King Haraldr, that you have not heard about the war between these two countries? Or do you think your luck so good that you will be able to bring valuable possessions to Denmark, while others cannot get there unmolested, even though they have pressing business?

Audunn answered: My Lord, that is for you to decide, but I shall agree to nothing other than that which I had already planned.

Then the King said: Why should we not have it like this, that you go your own way, just as you choose, and then visit me on your way back, and tell me how King Sveinn rewards you for the bear? It may be that luck will go with you.

I will promise you to do that, said Audunn.

Audunn now followed the coast southward and eastward into the Vik, and from there to Denmark, and by that time every penny of his money had been spent, and he had to beg food for himself as well as for the bear. He called on one of King Sveinn's stewards, a man named Aki, and asked him for some provisions, both for himself and for his bear.—I intend, said he, to give the bear to King Sveinn.

> Aki said that he would sell him some provisions if he liked, but Audunn answered that he had nothing to pay for them,—but yet, said he, I would like to carry out my plan, and to take the beast to the King.

Aki answered: I will supply such provisions as the two of you need until you go before the King, but in exchange I will have half the bear. You can look at it in this way: the beast will die on your hands, since you need a lot of provisions and your money is spent, and it will come to this, that you will have nothing out of the bear.

When Audunn considered this, it seemed to him that there was some truth in what the steward had said, and they agreed on these terms: he gave Aki half the bear, and the King was then to set a value on the whole.

Now they were both to visit the King, and so they did. They went into his presence and stood before his table. The King wondered who this man could be, whom he did not recognize, and then said to Audunn: Who are you?

Audunn answered: I am an Icelander, my Lord, and I came lately from Greenland, and now from Norway, intending to bring you this white bear. I gave all I had for him, but I have had a serious setback, so now I only own half of the beast.—Then Audunn told the King what had happened between him and the steward, Aki.

The King asked: Is that true, what he says, Aki?

True it is, said Aki.

The King said: And did you think it proper, seeing that I had placed you in a high position, to let and hinder a man who had taken it on himself to bring me a precious gift, for which he had given all he had? King Haraldr saw fit to let him go his way in peace, and he is no friend of ours. Think, then, how far this was honest on your part. It would be just to have you put to death, but I will not do that now; you must rather leave this land at once, and never come into my sight again. But to you, Audunn, I owe the same gratitude as if you were giving me the whole of the bear, so now stay here with me.

Audunn accepted the invitation and stayed with King Sveinn for a while.

II

After some time had passed Audunn said to the King: I desire to go away now, my Lord.

The King answered rather coldly: What do you want to do then, since you do not wish to stay with us?

Audunn answered: I wish to go south on a pilgrimage.

If you had not such a good end before you, said the King, I should be vexed at your desire to go away.

Now the King gave Audunn a large sum of silver, and he travelled south with pilgrims bound for Rome. The King arranged for his journey, asking him to visit him when he came

Audunn went on his way until he reached the city of Rome in the south. When he had stayed there as long as he wished, he turned back, and a severe illness attacked him, and he grew terribly emaciated. All the money which the King had given him for his pilgrimage was now spent, and so he took up his staff and begged his food. By now his hair had fallen out and he looked in a bad way. He got back to Denmark at Easter, and went to the place where the King was stationed. He dared not let the King see him, but stayed in a side-aisle of the church, intending to approach the King when he went to church for Nones. But when Audunn beheld the King and his courtiers splendidly arrayed, he did not dare to show himself.

When the King went to drink in his hall, Audunn ate his meal out of doors, as is the custom of Rome pilgrims, so long as they have not laid aside their staff and scrip. In the evening, when the King went to Vespers, Audunn intended to meet him, but shy as he was before, he was much more so now that the courtiers were merry with drink. As they were going back, the King noticed a man, and thought he could see that he had not the confidence to come forward and meet him. But as the courtiers walked in, the King turned back and said:

Let the man who wants to meet me come forward; I think there must be someone who does.

Then Audunn came forward and fell at the feet of the King, but the King hardly recognized him. As soon as he knew who he was, he took Audunn by the hand and welcomed him:—You have changed a lot since we met last,—he said, and then he led Audunn into the hall after him. When the courtiers saw Audunn they laughed at him, but the King said:

There is no need for you to laugh at this man, for he has provided better for his soul than you have.

The King had a bath prepared for Audunn and then gave him clothes, and now he stayed with the King.

III

It is told that one day in the spring the King invited Audunn to stay with him for good, and said he would make him his cup-bearer, and do him great honour.

Audunn answered: May God reward you, my Lord, for all the favours you would show me, but my heart is set on sailing out to Iceland.

The King said: This seems a strange choice to me,—but Audunn answered: My Lord, I cannot bear to think that I should be enjoying high honour here with you, while my mother is living the life of a beggar out in Iceland. For by now, all that I contributed for her subsistence before I left Iceland, has been used up.

The King answered: That is well spoken and like a man, and good fortune will go with you. This was the one reason for your departure which would not have offended me. So stay with me until the ships are made ready for sea.—And this Audunn did.

One day towards the end of spring King Sveinn walked down to the quay, where men were getting ships ready to sail to various lands, to the Baltic lands and Germany, to Sweden and Norway. The King and Audunn came to a fine vessel, and there were some men busy fitting her out. The King asked:

How do you like this ship, Audunn?

Audunn answered: I like her well, my Lord.

The King said: I will give you this ship and reward you for the white bear.

Audunn thanked the King for his gift as well as he knew how.

After a time, when the ship was quite ready to sail, King Sveinn said to Audunn:

If you wish to go now, I shall not hinder you, but I have heard that you are badly off for harbours in your country, and that there are many shelterless coasts, dangerous to shipping. Now, supposing you are wrecked, and lose your ship and your goods, there will be little to show that you have visited King Sveinn and brought him a precious gift.

Then the King handed him a leather purse full of silver: You will not be altogether penniless, said he, even if you wreck your ship, so long as you can hold on to this. But yet it may be, said the King, that you will lose this money, and then it will be of little use to you that you have been to see King Sveinn and given him a precious gift.

Then the King drew a ring from his arm and gave it to Audunn, saying: Even if it turns out so badly that you wreck your ship and lose your money, you will still not be a pauper if you reach land, for many men have gold about them in a shipwreck, and if you keep this ring there will be something to show that you have been to see King Sveinn. But I will give you this advice, said the King, do not give this ring away, unless you should feel yourself so much indebted to some distinguished man—then give the ring to him, for it is a fitting gift for a man of rank. And now farewell.

IV

After this Audunn put to sea and made Norway, and had his merchandise brought ashore, and that was a more laborious task than it had been last time he was in Norway. Then he went into the presence of King Haraldr, wishing to fulfil the promise he had given him before he went to Denmark. Audunn gave the King a friendly greeting, which he accepted warmly.

Sit down, said the King, and drink with us, and so Audunn did. Then King Haraldr asked: What reward did King Sveinn give you for the bear?

Audunn answered: This, my Lord, that he accepted him from me.

I would have given you that, said the King, but what else did he give you?

Audunn said: He gave me silver to make a pilgrimage
to Rome, but King Haraldr said:

King Sveinn gives many people silver for pilgrimages and for other things, even if they do not bring him valuable gifts. What more did he do for you?

He offered to make me his cup-bearer and to give me great honours.

That was a good offer, said the King, but he must have given you still more.

Audunn said: He gave me a merchantman with a cargo of wares most profitable for the Norway trade.

That was generous, said the King, but I would have rewarded you as well as that. Did he give you anything else?

Audunn said: He gave me a leather purse full of silver, and said that I would still not be penniless if I kept it, even if my ship were wrecked off Iceland.

The King said: That was magnificent, and more than I should have done. I would have thought my debt discharged if I had given you the ship. Did he give you anything else?

Certainly he gave me something else, my Lord, said Audunn; he gave me this ring which I am wearing on my arm, and said that I might chance to lose all my property, and yet not be destitute if I had this ring. But he advised me not to part with it unless I were under such an obligation to some noble man that I wished to give it to him. And now I have come to the right man, for it was in your power to take from me both my bear and my life, but you allowed me to go to Denmark in peace when others could not go there.

The King received the gift graciously and gave Audunn fine presents in exchange before they parted. Audunn laid out his merchandise on his voyage to Iceland, and sailed out that same summer, and people thought him the luckiest of men.

From this man Audunn was descended Thorsteinn Gyduson. [Footnote: Thorsteinn Gyduson was drowned in the year 1190. Unless interpolated, the allusion to him shows that the story was written after that date.]

EINAR H. KVARAN

A DRY SPELL

It had rained for a fortnight—not all the time heavily, but a fog had sullenly hung about the mountain tops, clinging to the atmosphere and rendering the whole of existence a dull gray colour. Every little while it would discharge a fine drizzle of rain or a heavy shower down upon the hay and everything else on earth, so that only the stones would occasionally be dry—but the grass never.

We were tired of the store—indeed, I should like to know who would have enjoyed it. It dated back to the beginning of the last century, a tarred, coal-black, ramshackle hut. The windows were low and small, the windowpanes diminutive. The ceiling was low. Everything was arranged in such a way as to exclude the possibility of lofty flights of thought or vision.

Just now, not a living soul looked in—not even those thriftless fellows who lived by chance jobs in the village and met in daily conclave at the store. We had often cursed their lengthy visits, but now that they had hired themselves out during the haymaking, we suddenly realized that they had often been entertaining. They had made many amusing remarks and brought us news of the neighbourhood. And now we cursed them for their absence.

We sat there and smoked, staring vacantly at the half-empty shelves, and all but shivering in the damp room. There was no heater in the store at any season, and the one in the office, if used, emitted spurts of smoke through every aperture except the chimney. It had not been cleaned since sometime during winter, and we were not ambitious enough for such an undertaking in the middle of the summer.

We tried to transfer our thoughts from the store to the world outside. We made clever comments to the effect that the farmers were now getting plenty of moisture for the hay-fields, and that it would be a pity if rain should set in now, right at the beginning of the haying season. We had nothing further to say on the subject, but this we repeated from day to day. In short, we were depressed and at odds with things in general. Until the dry spell.

One morning, about nine o'clock, the bank of fog began to move. First, there appeared an opening about the size of your hand, and through it the eastern sky showed a bright blue. Then another opening, and through it shone the sun.

We knew what this was called, and we said to each other: Merely a 'morning promise'—implying, nothing reliable. But it was more. The fog began to show thinner and move faster along the mountain ridge opposite. Then it gathered in a deep pass and lay there heaped up like newly carded, snowy wool. On either side, the mountains loomed a lovely blue, and in their triumph ignored the fog almost completely. When we ventured a look through the doorway of the store, there was nothing to be seen overhead save the clear, blue sky and the sunshine.

On the opposite shore of the fjord, the people looked to us like the cairns out on the moorlands, only these tiny cairns moved in single file about the hay-fields. I seemed to smell the sweet hay in the homefields, but of course this was only my imagination. I also fancied I could hear the maids laughing, especially one of them. I would willingly have sacrificed a good deal to be over there helping her dry the hay. But of this subject no more; I did not intend to write a love story—at least, not in the ordinary sense of the word.

The dry spell lasted. We, the clerks, took turns at staying out of doors as much as possible, and 'drinking deeply of the golden fount of sunshine'.

In the afternoon of the third day, I dropped in at the doctor's. I felt somewhat weary with walking—and idleness—and looked forward to the doctor's couch and conversation.

A cigar? asked the doctor.

Yes, a cigar, I answered. I have smoked only six today.

Beer or whisky and water? queried the doctor.

A small whisky, I replied.

I lit my cigar, inhaling deeply of its fragrance—then exhaling through mouth and nostrils. I sighed with contentment; the cigar was excellent.

Then we began to drink the whisky and water at our leisure. I reclined against the head of the couch, stretched out my feet, was conscious of a luxurious sensation—and sent my thoughts for a moment across the fjord, where they preferred to remain.

The doctor was in high spirits. He talked about the Japanese and Russians, the most recently discovered rays, and the latest disclosures on how is felt to die.

My favourite pastime is to listen to others speaking. I never seem able to think of any topics worthy of conversation myself, but I am almost inclined to say that my ability to listen amounts to an art. I can remain silent with an air of absorbing interest, and once in a while offer brief comment, not to set forth an opinion or display any knowledge—for I have none to spare—but merely to suggest new channels to the speaker and introduce variety, that he may not tire of hearing himself speak.

I felt extremely comfortable on the couch. I thought it particularly entertaining to hear the doctor tell how it felt to die. There is always something pleasantly exciting about death—when it is reasonably far away from you. It seemed so beautifully far away from the perfume of the tobacco-smoke, the flavour of whisky, and the restfulness of the couch, and when my mind wandered to her across the fjord—as wander it would in spite of my studied attention—then death seemed so far off shore that I could scarcely follow the description of how it felt to others to die.

In the midst of this dreamy contentment and deluge of information from the doctor, the door was somewhat hastily thrown open. I was looking the other way and thought it must be one of the doctor's children.

But it was old man Thordur from the Bend.

I knew him well. He was over fifty, tall and large-limbed, with a hoary shock of hair and a snub nose. I knew he had a host of children—I had been at his door once, and they had run, pattered, waddled, crept, and rolled through the doorway to gape at me. It had seemed as hopeless to try to count them as a large flock of sheep. I knew there was no income except what the old man and woman—and possibly the elder children—managed to earn from day to day. My employer in Copenhagen had strictly forbidden us to give credit to such—and of course he now owed us more than he would ever be able to pay.

He does not even knock—the old ruffian, I said to myself.

From his appearance, something was wrong. His face was unnaturally purplish, his eyes strangely shiny—yet dull withal. It even seemed to me that his legs shook under him.

Can it be that the old devil is tipsy—at the height of the haying season—and dry weather at that? I mentally queried.

The doctor evidently could not recall who he was.

Good-day to you, my man, he said, and what matter have you in hand?

I merely came to get those four crowns.

Which four crowns? asked the doctor.

Thordur raised his voice: The four crowns you owe me.

It was now evident that it was difficult for him to remain standing.

I felt assured that the old rascal had been drinking like a fish. I was surprised. I had never heard he was inclined that way. He lived out there on the hillside a short distance above the village. I began to wonder where he had been able to obtain so much liquor— certainly not from us at the store.

What is your name? asked the doctor.

My name? Don't you know my name? Don't you know me?—Thordur—Thordur of the Bend. I should best of all like to get the money at once.

Yes, that's so—you are Thordur of the Bend, said the doctor. And you are up? But listen, my good man, I owe you nothing. You owe me a small sum—but that does not matter in the least.

I care nothing about that, but I should best of all like to get the money at once, repeated Thordur.

May I feel your hand for a minute? said the doctor.

Thordur extended his hand, but it seemed to me that he did not know it. He looked off into space, as if thinking of other things—or rather as if he had no thoughts whatever. I saw the doctor's fingers on his wrist.

You are a sick man, he said.

Sick?—Yes—of course I am sick. Am I then to pay you four crowns? I haven't got them now.

It makes no difference about those four crowns, but why did you get up like this? Have you forgotten that I ordered you to remain in bed when I saw you the other day?

In bed?—How the devil am I to remain in bed? Tell me that!

You must not get up in this condition. Why, you are delirious!

What a fool you are—don't you know that there is a dry spell.

Yes, I AM aware of the dry spell.—It was evidently not quite clear to him what that had to do with the case.—Have a chair, and we will talk it over.

A chair? No!—Who, then, should dry the hay in the homefield? I had some of it cut when I was taken down—why do you contradict me? And the youngsters have made some attempts at it—but who is to see about drying it?—Not Gudrun—she can't do everything. The youngsters?—what do they know about drying hay?—Who, then, is to do it?—Are YOU going to do it?

Something will turn up for you, said the doctor, somewhat at a loss.

Something will turn up? Nothing has ever turned up for ME.

Cold shivers passed through me. His remark rang true: I knew that nothing had ever turned up for him. I felt faint at looking into such an abyss of hopelessness. Instantly I saw that the truth of this delirious statement concerned me more than all the wisdom of the ages.

Do I get those four crowns you owe me?—Thordur asked. He was now trembling so that his teeth chattered.

The doctor produced four crowns from his purse and handed them to him. Thordur laid them on the table and staggered towards the door.- -You are leaving your crowns behind, man, said the doctor.

I haven't got them now, said Thordur, without looking back and still making his way towards the door.—But I'll pay them as soon as I can.

Isn't there a vacant bed upstairs at the store? inquired the doctor.

Yes, I answered. We will walk with you down to the store, Thordur.

Walk with me?—Be damned!—I am off for the hay-field.

We followed him outside and watched him start out. After a short distance he tumbled down. We got him upstairs in the store.

A few days later he could have told us, if anyone had been able to communicate with him, whether they are right or wrong, those latest theories on how it feels to die.

—But who dries the hay in his homefield now?

Guðmundur Friðjónsson

THE OLD HAY

During the latter part of the reign of King Christian the Ninth, there lived at Holl in the Tunga District a farmer named Brandur. By the time the events narrated here transpired, Brandur had grown prosperous and very old—old in years and old in ways. The neighbours thought he must have money hidden away somewhere. But no one knew anything definitely, for Brandur had always been reserved and uncommunicative, and permitted no prying in his house or on his possessions. There was, however, one thing every settler in those parts knew: Brandur had accumulated large stores of various kinds. Anyone passing along the highway could see that.

Brandur usually had some hay remaining in lofts and yards when spring came, and, besides, there was the immense stack that stood on a knoll out in the homefield before the house. It had been there for many years and was well protected against wind and weather by a covering of sod. Brandur had replenished the hay, a little at a time, by using up that from one end only and filling in with fresh hay the following summer.

Brandur was hospitable to such guests as had business with him, and refused to accept payment for food or lodging; but very few people ever came to see him, and these were mostly old friends with whom he had financial dealings. Brandur was willing to make loans against promissory notes and the payment of interest. There were not many to whom he would entrust his money, however, and he never lost a penny. Whenever these callers came, he would bring out the brandy bottle.

The buildings at Holl were all in a tumble-down state; the furniture was no better. There wasn't a chair in the whole house; even the baðstofa had only a dirt floor, and it was entirely unsheathed on the inside except for a few planks nailed on the wall from the bed up as far as the rafters. The clock was the sole manufactured article in the room. But friends of the old man knew that underneath his bed he kept a fairly large carved wooden chest, bearing the inscription anno 1670. The chest was heavy and was always kept locked. Only the nearest of kin had ever seen its contents.

Brandur was not considered obliging; it was very difficult to get to see him. Yet he was willing to sell food at any time for cash; hay, too, as long as there was still some remaining in his lofts. He would also sell hay against promises of lambs, especially wethers, once it was certain that the cold of winter was past. But his old haystack he refused to touch for anyone.

In this way Brandur stumbled down the pathway of life until he lost his sight. Even then, he was still sound in mind and body. While his vision remained unimpaired, it had been his habit to walk out to the old haystack every day and stroll around it slowly, examining it carefully from top to bottom and patting it with his hands. This habit he kept up as long as the weather permitted him to be outdoors, and he did not give it up even after his sight was gone. He would still take his daily walk out to the haystack on the knoll, drag himself slowly around it, groping with his hands to feel it, as if he wished to make sure that it still stood there, firm as a rock and untouched. He would stretch out his hands and touch its face and count the strips of turf to himself in a whisper.

Brandur still tilled the land, though he kept but little help and was living chiefly on the fruits of his former labours. He had fine winter pastures, and good meadows quite near the house, from which the hay could easily be brought in. The old man steadfastly refused to adopt modern farming methods; he had never levelled off the hummocks, nor drained or irrigated the land. But he did hire a few harvest hands in the middle of the season, paying them in butter, tallow, and the flesh of sheep bellies. The wages he paid were never high, yet he always paid whatever had been agreed upon.

Old Brandur had been blessed with only one child, a daughter named Gudrun. who had married a farmer in the district. Since his daughter's marriage, Brandur kept a housekeeper and one farm hand, a young man whom Brandur had reared and who, it was rumoured, was his natural son. But that has nothing to do with the story.

When Brandur had reached a ripe old age, there came a winter with much frost and snow. Time and again, some of the snow and ice would thaw, but then a hard frost would come, glazing everything in an icy coating. This went on until late in April. By that time, almost every farmer in the district had used up his hay; every one of them was at the end of his store, and nowhere was there a blade of grass to feed the live-stock, for the land still lay frozen under its blanket of hard-packed snow and ice. When things had come to this pass, a general district meeting was called to discuss the situation and decide what should be done. Brandur's son-in-law Jon was made chairman of the meeting.

During the discussion it was brought to light that many of the flocks would die of hunger unless 'God Almighty vouchsafed a turn in the weather very soon', or Old Brandur could be induced to part with his old hay. That stack would help, if properly divided among those who were in greatest need. The quantity of hay it contained was estimated, and the general opinion expressed that, if it were divided, the flocks of every farmer in the district could be fed for at least two weeks, even if they could not in that time be put out to pasture.

Jon being chairman of the District Council, as well as Brandur's son-in-law, it fell to his lot to go to the old man and ask for the hay.

So it came about that, on his way home from the meeting, Jon stopped at Holl. The day was cold and clear, the afternoon sun shining down upon the snow-covered landscape. The icy blanket turned back the rays of warmth as if it would have nothing to do with the sun. But wherever rocks and gravelly banks protruded, the ice appeared to be peeled off, for in those spots the sun's rays had melted it, though only at mid-day and on the south. All streams and waterfalls slumbered in silence under the snowy blanket. A chill silence reigned over the whole valley. Not a bird was to be seen, not even a snow bunting, only two ravens which kept flying from farmhouse to farmhouse, and even their cawing had a hungry note.

When Jon rode up to the house at Holl, he found Brandur out by the haystack. The old man was carefully groping his way around the stack, feeling it on all sides and counting the strips of turf in so loud a voice that Jon could hear him: O-n-e, t-w-o, three.

Jon dismounted and, going over to Brandur, saluted him with a kiss.

How are you? God bless you, said Brandur. And who may this be?

Jon of Bakki, replied the visitor.—Gudrun sends greetings.

Ah, yes. And how is my Gunna? Is she well?

She was well when I left home this morning. Now I am on my way back from the meeting that was held to discuss the desperate situation— you must have heard about it.

Yes, certainly. I've heard about it. I should say so! One can't get away from talk of hay shortage and hard times. That is quite true. Any other news?

Nothing worth mentioning, answered Jon. Nothing but the general hard times and hay shortage. Every farmer at the end of his tether, or almost there, no one with as much as a wisp of hay to spare, and only a few likely to make out till Crouchmas without aid.

Too bad! said Brandur. Too bad! And he blew out his breath, as though suffocating from strong smoke or bad air.

For a while there was silence, as if each mistrusted the other and wondered what was in the air. Brandur stood there with one hand resting on the haystack, while he thrust the other into his trousers pocket, or underneath the flap of his trousers. He always wore the old-fashioned trousers with a flap, in fact had never possessed any other kind. Meanwhile, holding the reins, Jon stood there gazing at the hay and making a mental estimate of it. Then he turned to his father-in-law and spoke:

The purpose of my visit to you, my dear Brandur, is to ask that you let us have this hay—this fine old hay that you have here. The District Council will, of course, pay you; the parish will guarantee payment. We have discussed that matter fully.

When Jon ceased speaking, Brandur blew the air from his mouth in great puffs, as though deeply stabbed by a sharp pain in the heart. For a while he held his peace. Then he spoke:

Not another word! Not another word! What's this I hear? My hay for the district? My hay to supply all the farmers in the district? Do you think for one moment that this little haystack is enough to feed all the flocks in the whole district? Do you think this tiny haycock will be enough for a whole parish? I think not!

But we have calculated it, protested Jon. We have estimated that the hay in this stack will be enough to feed the flocks in the district for about two weeks, if a little grain is used with it, and if the hay is distributed equally among the farmers who need it most. There may be enough for three weeks, should it turn to be as much as or more than I expect. By that time, we surely hope, the season will be so far advanced that the weather will have changed for the better.

So! You have already estimated the amount of hay in my stack! said Brandur. You have already divided this miserable haycock among yourselves, divided it down to the very last straw. And you have weighed it almost to a gram. Then why speak to me about it? Why not take it just as it is and scatter it to the four winds? Why not?— The voice of the old man shook with anger.

No, said Jon. We will not do that. We want to ask your permission first. We had no intention of doing otherwise; we intended to ask you for the hay. And we did not mean to vex you, but rather to honour you in this manner. Is it not an honour to be asked to save a whole district from ruin?

Oh, so all this is being done to honour me! said the old man, roaring with laughter. Perhaps you believe me to be in my second childhood. Not at all! Old Brandur can still see beyond the tip of his nose.

The cold-heartedness shown by the old man's laughter at the distress of his fellowmen roused Jon's ire. He could see nothing laughable about the desperate situation in the district.

Are you then going to refuse to let us have the hay, refuse to sell it at full price, with the Parish Council guaranteeing payment? he asked in a tone that was angry, yet under perfect control?—Is that your final answer?

Yes, responded Brandur. That is my final answer. I will not let the tiny mouthful of hay I have here go while there is still life in my body, even though you mean to insure payment, and even though you actually do guarantee payment. After all, who among you will be in a position to guarantee payment if all the flocks die? The cold weather may not let up until the first of June or even later. In that case the sheep will all die. It won't go very far, this tiny haycock, not for so many. It will not, I tell you.

But what are you going to do with the hay? If everyone else loses his flocks, everyone but you, what enjoyment will there be in owning it? And what benefit? asked Jon.

That does not concern me! replied the old man. That concerns them. It was they who decided the size of the flocks they undertook to feed this winter, not I. Besides, they could have cut as much hay as I did, even more, for they still have their eyesight. Their failure is due to their own laziness and bad judgment. That's what ails them! Ruins them!

But you won't be able to take this great big haystack with you into the life eternal, said Jon. The time is coming when you will have to part with it. Then it will be used as the needs require. And what good will it do you? What are you going to do with it?

I am going to keep it, answered Brandur. I intend to keep it right here on the knoll, keep it in case the haying should be poor next summer. There may be a poor growth of grass and a small hay crop; there may be a volcanic eruption and the ashes may poison the grass, as they have done in former years. Now, do you understand me?

So saying, Brandur tottered off towards the house to indicate that the conversation was at an end. His countenance was as cold as the sky in the evening after the sun has set, and the hard lines in it resembled the streaks in the ice on rocks and ledges where the sun's rays had shone that day and laid bare the frozen ground.

Brandur entered the house, while Jon mounted again. They scarcely said a word of farewell, so angry were they both.

Jon's horse set off at a brisk pace, eager to reach home, and galloped swiftly over the hard, frozen ground. After the sun had gone down, the wind rose and a searing cold settled over the valley, whitening Jon's moustache where his breath passed over it.

Jon's anger grew as he sped along. Naturally hightempered, he had lately had many reasons for anger since he took over his official duties. The people in his district were like people the world over: they blamed the Board constantly, accusing it of stupidity and favouritism. Yet most of them paid their taxes reluctantly and only when long overdue. Sometimes they were almost a year in arrears.

Jon reviewed the matter of the hay in his mind, also the other vexations of the past. He was sick and tired of all the trouble. And now the life of the whole district hung on a thin thread, the fate of which depended upon the whims of the weather. Jon's nose and cheekbones smarted from the cold; his shoes were frozen stiff, and pinched his feet, and his throat burned with the heat of anger rising from his breast.

Jon was rather quiet when he reached home that evening, although he did tell his wife of his attempt to deal with her father.

Yes, said Gudrun, papa sets great store by that hay. He cannot bear to part with it at any price. That is his nature.

Tomorrow you must go, Jon told her, and try to win the old man over in some way. I'd hate to be obliged to take the hay from him by force, but that will be necessary if everything else fails.

The following day Gudrun went to see her father. The weather still remained cold. When Gudrun dismounted before the house at Holl, there was no one outside to greet her or announce her arrival, and so she entered, going straight into the baðstofa. There she found her father sitting on his bed, knitting a seaman's mitten, crooning an old ditty the while:

Far from out the wilderness
Comes raging the cold wind;
And the bonds of heaven's king
It doth still tighter bind.

Gudrun leaned over her father and kissed him.

Is that you, Gunna dear? he asked.

Yes papa, she said, at the same time slipping a flask of brandy into the bosom of his shirt.

This greatly pleased the old man.

> Gunna dear, he said, you always bring me something to cheer me up.
> Not many nowadays take the trouble to cheer the old man. No indeed.
> Any news? It's so long since you have been to see me, a year or more.

No news everyone hasn't heard: hard times, shortage of hay, and worry everywhere. That is only to be expected. It's been a hard winter, the stock stall-fed for so long, at least sixteen weeks, on some farms twenty.

Quite true, said Brandur. It's been a cold winter, and the end is not yet. The cold weather may not break up before the first of June, or even Midsummer Day. The summer will be cold, the hay crop small, and the cold weather will probably set in again by the end of August, then another cold hard winter, and ...

He meant to go on, foretelling yet worse things to come, but Gudrun broke in: Enough of that, father. Things can't be as bad as that It would be altogether too much. I hope for a change for the better with the new moon next week, and mark you, the new moon rises in the southwest and on a Monday; if I remember right, you always thought a new moon coming on a Monday brought good weather.

I did, conceded Brandur. When I was a young man, a new moon coming on a Monday was generally the very best kind of moon. But like everything else, that has changed with the times. Now a Monday new moon is the worst of all, no matter in what quarter of the heavens it appears, if the weather is like this—raging sad carrying on so; that is true.

But things are in a pitiful state, said Gudrun, what with the hay shortage, almost everyone is badly off, and not a single farmer with a scrap of hay to spare, except you, papa.

Yes, I! answered Brandur. I, a poor, blind, decrepit old man! But what of you? Jon has enough hay, hasn't he? How is that? Doesn't he have enough?

Yes, we do have enough for ourselves, admitted Gudrun. But we can't hold onto it. Jon lends it to those in need until it is all gone and there is none left for us. He thinks of others as well as of himself.

What nonsense! What sense is there in acting like that? Every man for himself, said the old man.

That's right. But for us that is not enough. Jon is in a position where he must think of others; he has to think of all the farmers in the district—and small thanks he gets for his pains. He is so upset, almost always on tenterhooks. He didn't sleep a wink last night—was almost beside himself. He takes it so hard.

So Jon couldn't sleep a wink last night! repeated Brandur. Why be so upset? Why lie awake nights worrying about this? That doesn't help matters any. It isn't his fault that they are all on the brink of ruin.

Quite true, answered Gudrun. He is not to blame for that, and lying awake nights doesn't help matters, but that is Jon's disposition. He's tired to death of all the work for the Council and the everlasting fault-finding. He has had to neglect his own farm since he took up these public duties—and nothing for his time and trouble. Now this is too much. He is dead tired of it all, and so am I. In fact, I know it was worry about all this that kept Jon awake last night. We have been thinking of getting away from it all when spring comes and going to America.

Do you side with him in this? asked Brandur, grasping his daughter by the arm. Do you, too, agree to his giving away the hay you need for your own flocks, giving it away until you haven't enough for yourselves? Do you, too, want to go to America, away from your father who now has one foot in the grave?

Yes, I do, Gudrun replied. As a matter of fact, the plan was originally mine. If our flocks die, there will be no alternative; but if our sheep live and those of the neighbours die, our life will not be worth living because of the poverty and want round about us. Yes, papa, it was I suggested our going. I could see no other way out.

On hearing this, Brandur's mood softened somewhat. I expected to be allowed to pass my last days with you and your children, he said. I cannot go on living in this fashion any longer.

Pass your last days with us! exclaimed Gudrun. Have you, then, thought of leaving Holl? Have you planned to come and live with us? You've never said a word of this to me.

I have no intention of leaving Holl. That I have never meant to do. But that is not necessary. I thought you might perhaps be willing to move over here and live with me. I could then let you have what miserable little property I have left, Gunna, my dear.

And what about the hay, papa? Will you turn the hay over to us, the hay in the old stack? Everything depends on that.

The hay! The hay! the old man said. Still harping on the hay—the hay which doesn't amount to anything and cannot be of any real help. It's sheer nonsense to think that the hay in that stack is enough to feed the flocks of a whole district. There is no use talking about it I will not throw that tiny mouthful to all the four winds. It will do no good if divided among so many, but it is a comfort to me, to me alone. No, I will not part with it as long as there is a spark of life in me. That I will not, my love.

Brandur turned pale and the lines in his face became hard and rigid. Looking at him, Gudrun knew from experience that he was not to be shaken in his determination when in this mood. His face was like a sky over the wilderness streaked with threatening storm clouds.

Gudrun gave up. The tears rushed to her eyes, as she twined her arms around her father's neck and said: Goodbye, papa. Forgive me if I have angered you. I shall not come here again.

The old man felt the teardrops on his face, the heavy woman's tears, hot with anger and sorrow.

Gudrun dashed out of the room and mounted. Brandur was left alone in the darkness at mid-day. Yet in his mind's eye he could see the haystack out on the knoll. He rose and went out to feel it. It was still there. Gudrun had not ridden away with it. Brandur could hear the horseshoes crunching the hard, frozen ground as Gudrun rode off. He stood motionless for a long time, listening to the hoof beats. Then he went into the house.

Brandur felt restless. He paced the floor awhile, stopped for a moment to raise to his lips the flask his daughter had brought him, and drained it at one gulp. All that day he walked the floor, fighting with himself until night fell.

Then he sent his foster-son with a message to his daughter. Jon, he said, had his permission to haul the hay away the very next day, but it was all to be removed in one day; there was not to be a scrap of hay or a lump of sod left by evening.

But the weather changes quickly, says an old Icelandic adage. By morning, the weather had turned its spindle and the wind shifted to the south. Jon sent no message to anyone, nor did he proclaim that the old hay was available. He first wished to see what the thaw would amount to. By the following day, the whole valley was impassable because of slush and water, and the patches of earth appearing through the snowy blanket grew larger almost hourly.

Meanwhile, Brandur roamed through the house all day long, asking if anyone had come.—Aren't they going to take away these miserable hay scraps? About time they came and got them!—He seemed eager that the hay be removed at once.

That day he did not take his usual walk out to the stack to feel the hay. In fact, after that no one ever saw him show attachment to the old hay. His love of it seemed to have died the moment he granted his son-in-law permission to take it away.

That spring Brandur gave up housekeeping and of his own volition turned over the farm to his daughter and son-in-law. With them he lived to enjoy many years of good health. Never again did he take his daily walk out to the haystack to feel the hay. But he was able to take his sip of brandy to his dying day and repeat to himself the word of God—hymns and verses from the Bible.

Now he has passed on to eternity. But his memory lives like a stone- -a large, moss-covered stone by the wayside.

Jón TRAUSTI

WHEN I WAS ON THE FRIGATE

I was stormbound in the fishing village. I had come there by steamer, but now the steamer was gone and I was left behind there, a stranger, at a loss what to do.

My idea was to continue my journey overland, and my route lay for the most part through the mountainous country on the other side of the fjord. I hadn't managed to hire horses or a guide, and it was no easy matter to find one's own way in such stormy weather when the rivers were running in full flood. This was in the spring-time, round about the beginning of May.

I was staying at the home of the local doctor, who had given me shelter and who was now trying to help me in every way he could. He was in my room with me, and we were both sitting there, smoking cigars and chatting together. I had given up all hope of continuing my journey that day and was making myself comfortable on the doctor's sofa. But when we least expected it, we heard the sound of heavy sea-boots clumping along the corridor, and there was a knock at the door.

Come in, said the doctor. The door opened slowly, and a young man in seamen's clothes stood in the doorway.

I was asked to tell you that old Hrolfur from Weir will take that chap over there across in his boat, if he likes, said the man, addressing himself to the doctor.

We both stood up, the doctor and I, and walked towards the door.

That possibility hadn't occurred to either of us.

Is old Hrolfur going fishing then? asked the doctor.

Yes, he's going out to the islands and staying there about a week. It won't make any difference to him to slip ashore at Muladalir, if it would be any help.

That's fine, said the doctor, turning to me. It's worth thinking over, unless you really need to go round the end of the fjord. It'll save you at least a day on your journey, and it'll be easier to get horses and a man in Muladalir than it is here.

This was all so unexpected that I didn't quite know what to say. I looked at the doctor and the stranger in turn, and my first thought was that the doctor was trying to get rid of me. Then it occurred to me what a fine thing it would be to avoid having to cross all those rivers which flow into the head of the fjord. Finally I decided that the doctor had no ulterior motive and that his advice was prompted by sheer goodwill.

Is old Hrolfur all right at the moment? the doctor asked the man in the doorway.

Yes, of course he is, said the man.

All right? I said, looking at them questioningly. I thought that was a funny thing to ask.

The doctor smiled.

He's just a bit queer—up here, he said, pointing to his forehead.

The thought of having to set out on a long sea journey with a man who was half crazy made me shudder. I am certain, too, that the doctor could see what I was thinking, for he smiled good-naturedly.

Is it safe to go with him then? I asked.

Oh yes, quite safe. He's not mad, far from it. He's just a bit queer—he's got 'bats in the belfry', as men say. He gets these attacks when he's at home in the dark winter days and has nothing to occupy him. But there's little sign of it in the summer. And he's a first-class seaman.

Yes, a first-class seaman who never fails, said the man in the doorway. It's quite safe to go on board with him now. You can take my word for that.

Are you going with him? asked the doctor.

Yes, there's a crew of three with him. There'll be four of us in the boat altogether.

I looked at the man in the doorway—he was a young man of about twenty, promising and assured. I liked the look of him, very much.

Secretly I began to be ashamed of not daring to cross the fjord with three men such as he, even though the skipper was 'a bit queer in the head'.

Are you going to-day? said the doctor. Don't you think it's blowing a bit hard?

I don't think old Hrolfur'll let that bother him, said the man and smiled.

Can you use your sails?

Yes, I think so—there's a fair wind.

It was decided that I should go with them. I went to get ready as quickly as possible, and my luggage, saddle and bridle, were carried down to the boat.

The doctor walked to the jetty with us.

There, in the shelter of the breakwater, was old Hrolfur's boat, its mast already stepped, with the sail wrapped round it. It was a four- oared boat, rather bigger than usual, tarred all over except for the top plank, which was painted light blue. In the boat were the various bits of equipment needed for shark-fishing, including a thick wooden beam to which were attached four hooks of wrought iron, a keg of shark-bait which stank vilely, and barrels for the shark's liver. There were shark knives under the thwarts and huge gaffs hooked under the rib-boards. The crew had put the boxes containing their food and provisions in the prow.

In the stern could be seen the back of a man bending down. He was arranging stones in the well of the boat. He was dressed in overalls made of skin, which reached up to his armpits and which were fastened by pieces of thin rope crossing over his shoulders. Further forward there was a second man, and a third was up on the jetty.

Good day to you, Hrolfur, said the doctor.

Good day to you, grunted Hrolfur as he straightened himself up and spat a stream of yellowish-brown liquid from his mouth. Hand me that stone over there.

These last words were addressed not to the doctor or me, but to the man on the jetty. Hrolfur vouchsafed me one quick, unfriendly glance, but apart from that scarcely seemed to notice me. The look in those sharp, haunting eyes went through me like a knife. Never before had anyone looked at me with a glance so piercing and so full of misgiving.

He was a small man, and lively, though ageing fast. The face was thin, rather wrinkled, dark and weather-beaten, with light untidy wisps of hair round the mouth. I was immediately struck by a curious twitching in his features, perhaps a relic of former bouts of drinking. Otherwise his expression was harsh and melancholy. His hands were red, swollen and calloused as if by years of rowing.

Don't you think it's blowing rather hard, Hrolfur? asked the doctor after a long silence.

Oh, so-so, answered Hrolfur, without looking up.

Again there was silence. It was as if Hrolfur had neither time nor inclination for gossiping, even though it was the district medical officer talking to him.

The doctor looked at me and smiled. I was meant to understand that this was exactly what he had expected.

After another interval the doctor said: You are going to do this traveller a favour then, Hrolfur?

Oh, well, the boat won't mind taking him.

In other words, I was to be nothing but so much ballast.

> Don't you think it's going to be tricky landing there in
> Mular Creek?

Hrolfur straightened up, putting his hand to his back.

Oh, no, damn it, he said. There's an offshore wind and the sea's not bad, and anyway we'll probably get there with the incoming tide.

It isn't going to take you out of your way? I asked.

We won't argue about that. We'll get there all the same. We often give ourselves a rest in the old creek when we have to row.

Immediately afterwards I said good-bye to the doctor and slid down into the boat. The man on the jetty cast off, threw the rope down into the boat and jumped in after it.

One of the crew thrust the handle of an oar against the breakwater and pushed off. Then they rowed for a short spell to get into the wind, whilst old Hrolfur fixed the rudder.

The sail filled out; the boat heeled gently over and ran in a long curve. The islets at the harbour mouth rushed past us. We were making straight for the open bay.

On the horizon before us the mountainous cliffs, dark blue with a thick, ragged patch of mist at the top, towered steeply over the waves. In between, the sea stretched out, seemingly for miles.

Hrolfur was at the rudder. He sat back in the stern on a crossbeam flush with the gunwale, his feet braced against the ribs on either side and in his hands the rudder lines, one on each side, close to his thighs.

I was up with the crew near the mast. We all knew from experience that Icelandic boats sailed better when well-loaded forward. All four of us were lying down on the windward side, but to leeward the foam still bubbled up over the rowlocks.

If you think we're not going fast enough, lads, you'd better start rowing—but no extra pay, said old Hrolfur, grinning.

We all took his joke well, and I felt that it brought me nearer to the old man; up to then I'd been just a little scared of him. A joke is always like an outstretched hand.

For a long time we hardly spoke. In front of the mast we lay in silence, whilst old Hrolfur was at the stern with the whole length of the boat between us.

The crew did all they could to make me comfortable. I lay on some soft sacking just in front of the thwart and kept my head under the gunwale for protection. The spray from the sea went right over me and splashed down into the boat on the far side.

The boy who had come for me to the doctor's settled himself down in the bows in front of me. His name was Eric Ericsson, and the more I saw of him the more I liked him.

The second member of the crew sat crosswise over the thwart with his back to the mast. He too was young, his beard just beginning to grow, red-faced, quiet and rather indolent-looking. He seemed completely indifferent, even though showers of spray blew, one after another, straight into his face.

The third member of the crew lay down across the boat behind the thwart; he put a folded oilskin jacket under his head and fell asleep.

For a long time, almost an hour, I lay in silence, thinking only of what I saw and heard around me. There was more than enough to keep me awake.

I noticed how the sail billowed out, full of wind, pulling hard at the clew-line, which was made fast to the gunwhale beside Hrolfur. The fore-sail resembled a beautifully curved sheet of steel, stiff and unyielding. Both sails were snow-white, semi-transparent and supple in movement, like the ivory sails on the model ships in Rosenborg Palace. The mast seemed to bend slightly and the stays were as taut as fiddle-strings. The boat quivered like a leaf. The waves pounded hard against the thin strakes of the boat's side. I could feel them on my cheek, though their dampness never penetrated; but in between these hammer blows their little pats were wonderfully friendly. Every now and then I could see the white frothing of the wave-crests above the gunwale, and sometimes under the sail the horizon was visible but, more often, there was nothing to be seen but the broad back of a wave, on which, for a time, the boat tossed before sinking down once more. The roll was scarcely noticeable, for the boat kept at the same angle all the time and cleft her way through the waves. The motion was comfortable and soothing to the mind; quite unlike the violent lunging of bigger ships.

Gradually the conversation came to life again. It was Eric who proved to be the most talkative, though the man on the thwart also threw in a word here and there.

We began to talk about old Hrolfur.

We spoke in a low voice so that he shouldn't hear what we said. There was, indeed, little danger of his doing so—the distance was too great and the storm was bound to carry our words away; but men always lower their voices when they speak of those they can see, even though they are speaking well of them.

My eyes scarcely left old Hrolfur, and as the men told me more, my picture of him became clearer and clearer.

He sat there silent, holding on to the steering ropes and staring straight ahead, not deigning us a single glance.

The crew's story was roughly this.

He was born and bred in the village, and he had never left it. The croft which he lived in was just opposite the weir in the river which flowed through the village, and was named after it.

He went to sea whenever possible; fished for shark in the spring and for cod and haddock in the other seasons. He never felt so happy as when he was on the sea; and if he couldn't go to sea, he sat alone at home in the croft mending his gear. He never went down to the harbour for work like the other fishermen and never worked on the land. Humming away and talking to himself he fiddled about in his shed, around his boat-house or his croft, his hands all grubby with tar and grease. If addressed, he was abrupt and curt in his answers, sometimes even abusive. Hardly anyone dared go near him.

Yet everyone liked him really. Everyone who got to know him said that he improved on acquaintance. His eccentricity increased as he grew older, but particularly after he had lost his son.

His son was already grown-up and had been a most promising young fellow. He was thought to be the most daring of all the skippers in the village and always went furthest out to sea; he was also the most successful fisherman of them all. But one day a sudden storm had caught them far out to sea, well outside the mouth of the fjord. Rowing hard, in the teeth of wind and tide, they managed to reach the cliffs, but by that time they were quite exhausted. Their idea had been to land at Mular Creek, but unfortunately their boat overturned as they tried to enter. Hrolfur's son and one other on board had been drowned, though the rest were saved.

After the disaster Hrolfur ignored everybody for a long time. It wasn't that he wept or lost heart. Perhaps he had done so for the first few days, but not afterwards. He just kept to himself. He took not the slightest notice of his wife and his other children, just as if they were no longer his concern. It was as though he felt he'd lost everything. He lived all alone with his sorrow and talked of it to no one. Nobody tried to question him; no one dared try to comfort him. Then, one winter, he started talking to himself.

Day and night, for a long time, he talked to himself, talked as though two or more men were chatting together, changing his tone of voice and acting in every way as though he were taking part in a lively and interesting conversation. There was nothing silly in what he said, although the subject matter was often difficult to follow. He would always answer if anyone spoke to him, slowly to be sure, but always sensibly and agreeably. Often, before he could answer, it was as though he had to wake up as from a sleep, and yet his work never suffered from these bouts of absentmindedness.

He never talked about his son. The conversations he held with himself were mostly concerned with various adventures he thought had befallen him; some were exaggerated, others pure invention. Sometimes he would talk of things he was going to do in the future, or things he would have done or ought to have in the past, but never about the present.

It wasn't long before the rumour spread that old Hrolfur was crazy, and for a long time hardly anyone dared to go to sea with him.

Now, that's all a thing of the past, said Eric and smiled. Nowadays there are always more who would like to go with him than he can take.

And does he catch plenty of fish?

Yes, he rarely fails.

Isn't he quite well-off then?

I don't know. At any rate he's not dependent on anyone else, and he's the sole owner of his boat and tackle.

He's rolling in money, the old devil, said the man at the mast, wiping the spray from his face with his hand.

Then they began to tell me about Mular Island and the life they would lead there in the coming week.

The island was a barren rock beyond the cliffs, and, in the autumn storms, was almost covered by the waves. The first thing they'd have to do, when they arrived, was to rebuild their refuge from the year before, roof it over with bits of driftwood and cover them with seaweed. That was to be their shelter at night, no matter what the weather. Nature had provided a landing-place, so that they'd no trouble with that, though the spot was so treacherous that one of them would have to stand watch over the boat every night.

Each evening they would row off from the island with their lines to some well-known fishing bank, for it was after midnight that the shark was most eager to take the bait. Savouring in his nostrils the smell of horse flesh soaked in rum and of rotten seal blubber, he would rush on the scent and greedily swallow whatever was offered. When he realised the sad truth that a huge hook with a strong barb was hidden inside this tempting dish and that it was no easy matter to disgorge the tasty morsel, he would try to gnaw through the shaft of the hook with his teeth. Very occasionally he might succeed, but usually his efforts failed. Attached to the hook was a length of strong iron chain; and sometimes, though defeated by the hook, he would manage to snip through the chain. Then, in his joy at being free, this creature with the magnificent appetite would immediately rush to the next hook, only to be caught there when the lines were drawn in. If the shark failed in his efforts to gnaw himself free, he would try, by twisting and turning, to break either the hook or the chain; but man had foreseen this possibility and had made the hook to turn with him. With exemplary patience 'the grey one' would continue his twisting until he had been drawn right up to the side of the boat and a second hook made fast in him. His sea-green, light-shy, pig-like eyes would glare malevolently up at his tormentors, and in his maddened fury he would bite, snap and fight until he almost capsized the boat.

For centuries our forefathers had hunted the shark like this in open boats, but nowadays men preferred to use decked vessels. No one in the district still used the old method, apart from old Hrolfur.

He had dragged in many a 'grey one'. From the bottom of the boat Eric picked up one of the hooks and passed it to me; it was of wrought iron, half an inch thick, with a point of cast steel. But the spinning joint was almost chewed through and the hook shaft bitten and gnawed—the 'grey one' had fought hard that time.

The crew told me so much about their fishing adventures that I longed to go to the island with them.

Suddenly Eric gave me a nudge.

The conversation stopped, and we all looked back at old Hrolfur.

Now he's talking to himself.

We all held our breath and listened.

Hrolfur sat like a statue, holding the rudder-lines. His eyes wore a far-away look and a curious smile of happiness played over his face.

After a short silence, he spoke again—in a perfectly normal voice.

When I was on the frigate—

For the time being that was all.

There was a touch of vanity in his smile, as though in memory of some old, half-ludicrous story from the past.

Yes, when I was on the frigate, my lad—

It was just as if there were someone sitting next to him beside the rudder, to whom he was relating his adventures.

Has he ever been on a warship? I whispered.

Never in his life, said Eric.

Our eyes never left him. I can still remember the curious twitching and working of his features. The eyes themselves were invisible; it was as though the man were asleep. But his forehead and temples were forever on the move, as if in mimicry of what he said.

I couldn't utter a sound. Everything was blurred before my eyes, for it was only then that the full realisation came upon me that the man at the rudder—the man who held all our lives in his hands—was half-crazed.

The crew nudged each other and chortled. They'd seen all this before.

She was running aground—heading straight for the reef,—a total loss, said Hrolfur, a total loss, I tell you. She was a beautiful craft, shining black and diced with white along the sides—ten fighting mouths on either side and a carved figure on her prow. I think the king would have been sorry to lose her. She was far too lovely to be ground to pieces there—they were glad when I turned up.

The crew did their best to smother their laughter.

'Top-sails up,' I shouted.—'Top-sails up, my lad.' The officer, for all his gold braid, went as pale as death. 'Top-sails up, in the devil's name.' The blue-jackets on the deck fell over themselves in fear. Yes, my lad, even though I hadn't a sword dangling by my side, I said, 'Top-sails up, in the devil's name.' And they obeyed me— they obeyed me. They didn't dart not to. 'Top-sails up, in the devil's name.'

Hrolfur raised himself up on the crossbeam, his fists clenched round the steering-ropes.

Eric was almost bursting with laughter and trying hard not to let it be heard; but the man at the mast made little attempt to stifle his.

She's made it, said Hrolfur, his face all smiles and nodding his head.— Out to sea. Straight out to sea. Let her lie down a bit, if she wants to. It'll do her no harm to ship a drop or two. Let it 'bubble up over her rowlocks,' as we Icelanders say. Even though she creaks a bit, it's all to the good. Her planks aren't rotten when they make that noise. All right, we'll sail the bottom out of her— but forward she'll go—forward, forward she shall go!

Hrolfur let his voice drop and drew out his jet words slowly.

By now we were far out in the fjord. The sea was rising and becoming more choppy because of tide currents. Good steering became more and more difficult. Hrolfur seemed to do it instinctively. He never once looked up and yet seemed to see all around him. He seemed to sense the approach of those bigger waves which had to be avoided or passed by. The general direction was never lost, but the boat ran wonderfully smoothly in and out of the waves—over them, before them and through them, as though she were possessed with human understanding. Not a single wave fell on her; they towered high above, advanced on her foaming and raging, but somehow—at the last moment—she turned aside. She was as sensitive as a frightened hind, quick to answer the rudder, as supple in her movements as a willing racehorse. Over her reigned the spirit of Hrolfur.

But Hrolfur himself was no longer there. He was 'on the frigate'. It was not his own boat he was steering in that hour, but a huge three- master with a whole cloud of sails above her and ten cannon on either side—a miracle of the shipwright's craft. The mainstays were of many-stranded steelwire, the halyards, all clustered together, struck at the mast and stays; they seemed inextricably tangled, and yet were in fact all ship-shape, taut and true, like the nerves in a human body. There was no need to steer her enormous bulk to avoid the waves or pass them by; it was enough to let her crush them with all her weight, let her grind them down and push them before her like drifts of snow. Groaning and creaking she ploughed straight on through all that came against her, heeling before the wind right down to her gunwale and leaving behind her a long furrow in the sea. High above the deck of this magnificent vessel, between two curved iron pillars, Hrolfur's boat hung like a tiny mussel shell.

Once upon a time this had been a dream of the future. But now that all hope of its fulfilment had been lost, the dream had long since become a reality. Hrolfur's adventure 'on the frigate' was a thing of the past.

For a long time he continued talking to himself, talked of how he had brought 'the frigate' safely to harbour, and how he had been awarded a 'gold medal' by the king. We could hear only anppets of this long rigmarole, but we never lost the drift of it. He spoke alternately in Danish and Icelandic, in many different tones of voice, and one could always tell, by the way he spoke, where he was in 'the frigate': whether he was addressing the crew on the deck, or the officers on the bridge, and when, his fantastic feat accomplished, he clinked glasses with them in the cabin on the poop.

The wind had slackened somewhat, but now that we had reached so far out into the bay the waves were higher; they were the remains of the huge ocean waves which raged on the high seas, remains which, despite the adverse wind, made their way far up the fjord.

Hrolfur no longer talked aloud, but he continued to hum quietly to himself. The crew around me began to doze off, and I think even I was almost asleep for a time. To tell the truth I wasn't very far from feeling seasick.

Soon afterwards the man who had been asleep in the space behind the mast rose to his feet, yawned once or twice, shook himself to restore his circulation and looked around.

It won't be long now before we get to Mular Creek, he said with his mouth still wide-open.

I was wide awake at once when I heard this, and raised myself up on my elbow. The mountain I had seen from the village—which then had been wrapped in a dark haze—now towered directly above us, rocky and enormous, with black sea-crags at its feet. The rocks were drenched with spray from the breakers, and the booming of the sea as it crashed into the basalt caves resounded like the roar of cannon.

There'll be no landing in the creek today, Hrolfur, the man said and yawned again. The breakers are too heavy.

Hrolfur pretended he hadn't heard.

Everybody aboard was awake now and watching the shore; and I think he was not the only one amongst us to shudder at the thought of landing.

On the mountain in front of us it was as though a panel was slowly moved to one side: the valleys of Muladalir opened up before us. Soon we glimpsed the roofs of the farms up on the hill-side. The beach itself was covered with rocks.

The boat turned into the inlet. It was quieter there than outside, and the sea was just a little another.

Loosen the foresail, Hrolfur ordered. It was Eric who obeyed and held on to the sheet Hrolfur himself untied the mainsail, whilst at the same time keeping hold of the sheet. I imagined Hrolfur must be thinking it safer to have the sails loose as it was likely to be gusty in the inlet.

Are you going to sail in? said the man who'd been asleep. His voice came through a nose filled with snuff.

Shut up, said Hrolfur savagely.

The man took the hint and asked no more questions. No one asked a question, though every moment now was one of suspense.

We all gazed in silence at the cliffs, which were lathered in white foam.

One wave after another passed under the boat. They lifted her high up, as if to show us the surf. As the boat sank slowly down into the trough of the wave, the surf disappeared and with it much of the shore. The wave had shut it out.

I was surprised how little the boat moved, but an explanation of the mystery was soon forthcoming: the boat and all she carried were still subject to Hrolfur's will.

He let the wind out of the mainsail and, by careful manipulation of the rudder, kept the boat wonderfully still. He was standing up now in front of the crossbeam and staring fixedly out in front of the boat. He was no longer talking to himself, he was no longer 'on the frigate', but in his own boat; he knew well how much depended on him.

After waiting for a while, watching his opportunity, Hrolfur suddenly let her go at full speed once more.

Now the moment had come—a moment I shall never forget—nor probably any of us who were in the boat with him. It was not fear that gripped us but something more like excitement before a battle. Yet, if the choice had been mine, we should have turned back from the creek that day.

Hrolfur stood at the rudder, immovable, his eyes shifting from side to side, now under the sail, now past it. He chewed vigorously on his quid of tobacco and spat. There was much less sign now of the twitchings round his eyes than there'd been earlier in the day, and his very calmness had a soothing effect on us all.

As we approached the creek, a huge wave rose up behind us. Hrolfur glanced at it with the corner of his eye. He spat and bared his teeth. The wave rose and rose, and it reached us just at the mouth of the creek, its overhanging peak so sharp as to be almost transparent. It seemed to be making straight for the boat.

As I watched, I felt the boat plummet down, as if the sea was snatched from under her; it was the undertow—the wave was drawing the waters back beneath it. By the gunwale the blue-green sea frothed white as it poured back from the skerries near the entrance to the creek.

The boat almost stood on end; it was as if the sea was boiling around us—boiling until the very seaweed on the rocks was turned to broth.

Suddenly an ice-cold lash, as of a whip, seemed to strike me in the face. I staggered forwards under the blow and grasped at one of the mainstays.

Let go the foresail, shouted Hrolfur.

When I was able to look up, the sails were flapping idly over the gunwale. The boat floated gently into the creek, thwart-deep in water.

We all felt fine.

It's true, I could feel the cold sea water dripping down my bare back, underneath my shirt, but I didn't mind. All that had happened to me was but a kiss, given me in token of farewell by the youngest daughter of the goddess of the waves.

The boat floated slowly in on the unaccustomed calm of the waters and stopped at the landing-place.

Standing there watching were two men from the farm.

I thought as much, it had to be old Hrolfur, one of them called out as we landed. It's no ordinary man's job to get into the creek on a day like this.

Hrolfur's face was wreathed in smiles: he made no answer, but slipping off the rudder in case it should touch bottom he laid it down across the stern.

We were given a royal welcome by the fanners from Mular, and all that I needed to further me on my journey was readily available and willingly granted. Nowhere does Iceland's hospitality flourish so well as in her outlying stations and in the remotest of her valleys, where travellers are few.

We all got out of the boat and pulled her clear of the waves. Every one of us was only too glad to get the opportunity of stretching his legs after sitting cramped up on the hard boards for nearly four hours.

I walked up to where old Hrolfur stood apart, on the low, flat rocks, thanked him for the trip and asked him what it cost.

Cost? he said, scarce looking at me. What does it cost? Just a minute now, my lad,—just a minute.

He answered me with the complete lack of formality one accords an old friend, though we had met for the first time that day. His whole face was scowling now, as he answered me brusquely—indeed, almost curtly; and yet there was something attractive about him, something that aroused both trust and respect and which made it impossible for me to resent his familiarity.

How much the trip costs? Just a minute now.

It seemed that his thoughts were elsewhere. He unloosened the brace of his overalls, reached down into the pocket of his patched garments beneath and, drawing out a fine length of chewing tobacco, took a bite. Then, breaking off a smallish length, he dropped it into the crown of his seaman's hat. Finally, slowly and very deliberately, he refastened the top of his overalls.

I expect you got a bit wet out there coming into the creek.

Oh, not really.

Sometimes one gets unpleasantly damp out there.

Hrolfur stood still, chewing his quid of tobacco and staring out at the entrance to the creek. He seemed to have forgotten all about answering my question.

Sometimes one gets unpleasantly damp out there, he repeated, laying great emphasis on every word. I looked straight at him and saw there were tears in his eyes. Now his features were all working again and twitching as they had done earlier.

There's many a boat filled up there, he added, and some have got no further. But I've floated in and out so far. Oh well, 'The silver cup sinks, but the wooden bowl floats on', as the proverb says. There was a time when I had to drag out of the water here a man who was better than me in every way—that's when I really got to know the old creek.

For a time he continued to stand there, staring out at the creek without saying a word. But, at last, after wiping the tears from his face with the back of his glove, he seemed to come to himself once more.

You were asking, my lad, what the journey costs—it costs nothing.

Nothing? What nonsense!

Not since you got wet, said Hrolfur and smiled, though you could still see the tears in his eyes. It's an old law of ours that if the ferry-man lets his passengers get wet, even though it's only their big toe, then he forfeits his toll.

I repeatedly begged Hrolfur to let me pay him for the journey, but it was no use. At last he became serious again and said:

The journey costs nothing, as I said to you. I've brought many a traveller over here to the creek and never taken a penny in return. But if you ever come back to our village again, and old Hrolfur should happen to be on land, come over to Weir and drink a cup of coffee with him—black coffee with brown rock-sugar and a drop of brandy in it; that is, if you can bring yourself to do such a thing.

This I promised him, and old Hrolfur shook me firmly and meaningfully by the hand as we parted.

> As they prepared to leave, we all three, the farmers from Mular and I, stood there on the rocks to see how Hrolfur would manage. The crew had furled the sails and sat down to the oars, whilst old Hrolfur stood in front of the crossbeam, holding the rudder-line.

They weren't rowing though, but held their oars up, waiting for their opportunity. All this while, wave after wave came riding through the entrance to the creek, pouring their white cascades of foam over the reefs.

Hrolfur watched them steadily and waited, like an animal ready to pounce on its prey.

Now, my lads, cried Hrolfur suddenly. The oars crashed into the sea, and the boat shot forward.

Just so, I thought, must the vikings in olden time have rowed to the attack.

Hrolfur's voice was lost to us in the roaring of the surf, but he seemed to be urging the men on to row their utmost. They rowed, indeed, like things possessed, and the boat hurtled forward.

At the mouth of the creek a surf-topped wave rose against them, sharp and concave, as it rushed on its way to the reefs. We held our breath. It was a terrifying but magnificent sight.

Hrolfur shouted something loudly, and at the same moment every oar hugged the side of the boat, like the fins of a salmon as it hurls itself at a waterfall. The boat plunged straight into the wave. For a moment we lost sight of her in the swirling spray; only the mast was visible. When we saw her again, she was well out past the breakers. She'd been moving fast and was well steered.

Hrolfur took his place on the crossbeam as if nothing had happened, just as he had sat there earlier in the day, whilst he was 'on the frigate'.

Two of the crew began to set the sails, whilst one started to bail out. Soon the boat was once more on the move.

I felt a strange lump in my throat as I watched old Hrolfur sailing away.

God bless you, old salt, I thought. You thoroughly deserved to cleave through the cold waters of Iceland in a shapely frigate.

The boat heeled over gracefully and floated over the waves like a gull with its wings outstretched. We stood there watching, without a move, until she disappeared behind the headland.

GUNNAR GUNNARSSON

FATHER AND SON

The two of them lived just outside the They were both called Snjolfur, and they usually distinguished as old Snjolfur and little Snjolfur. They themselves, however, addressed each other only as Snjolfur. This was a habit of long standing: it may be that, having the same name, they felt themselves bound still more firmly together by using it unqualified in this way. Old Snjolfur was something over fifty, little Snjolfur only just over twelve.

They were close together, the pair of them—each felt lost without the other. It had been like that ever since little Snjolfur could remember. His father could look further back. He remembered that thirteen years ago he had lived on his farm within easy riding distance of the village; he had a good wife and three sturdy and hopeful children.

Then his luck turned and one disaster after struck him. His sheep went down with pest, his cattle died of anthrax and other diseases. Then the children got whooping-cough and all three died, close enough together to lie in one grave. To pay his debts Snjolfur had to give up his farm and sell the land. Then he bought the land on the Point just outside the village, knocked up a cabin divided into two by a partition, and a fish-drying shed. When that was done, there was enough left to buy a cockle-shell of a boat. This was the sum of his possessions.

It was a poor and dismal life they led there, Snjolfur and his wife. They were both used to hard work, but they had had no experience of privation and constant care for the morrow. Most days it meant putting to sea if they were to eat, and it was not every night they went to bed with a full stomach. There was little enough left over for clothing and comfort.

Snjolfur's wife worked at fish-drying for the factor in the summer months, but good drying-days could not be counted on and the money was not much. She lived just long enough to bring little Snjolfur into the world, and the last thing she did was to decide his name. From then on, father and son lived alone in the cabin.

Little Snjolfur had vague memories of times of desperate misery. He had to stay at home through days of unrelieved torment and agony. There had been no one to look after him while he was too small to go off in the boat with his father, and old Snjolfur was forced to tie the boy to the bed-post to keep him out of danger in his absence. Old Snjolfur could not sit at home all the time: he had to get something to put in the pot.

The boy had more vivid memories of happier times, smiling summer days on a sea glittering in the sunshine. He remembered sitting in the stern and watching his father pulling in the gleaming fish. But even those times were mingled with bitterness, for there were days when the sky wept and old Snjolfur rowed out alone.

But in time little Snjolfur grew big enough to go off with his father, whatever the weather. From then on they contentedly shared most days and every night: neither could be without the other for more than a minute. If one of them stirred in his sleep, the other was awake on the instant; and if one could not get to sleep, the other did not close his eyes either.

One might think that it was because they had a lot to talk about that they were so wrapped up in each other. But that was not so. They knew each other so well and their mutual confidence was so complete that words were unnecessary. For days on end no more than scattered phrases fell between them; they were as well content to be silent together as to be talking together. The one need only look at the other to make himself understood.

Among the few words that passed between them, however, was one sentence that came up again and again—when old Snjolfur was talking to his son. His words were:

The point is to pay your debts to everybody, not owe anybody anything, trust in Providence.

In fact, father and son together preferred to live on the edge of starvation rather than buy anything for which they could not pay on the spot. And they tacked together bits of old sacking and patched and patched them so as to cover their nakedness, unburdened by debt.

Most of their neighbours were in debt to some extent; some of them only repaid the factor at odd times, and they never repaid the whole amount. But as far as little Snjolfur knew, he and his father had never owed a penny to anyone. Before his time, his father had been on the factor's books like everyone else, but that was not a thing he spoke much about and little Snjolfur knew nothing of those dealings.

It was essential for the two of them to see they had supplies to last them through the winter, when for many days gales or heavy seas made fishing impossible. The fish that had to last them through the winter was either dried or salted; what they felt they could spare was sold, so that there might be a little ready money in the house against the arrival of winter. There was rarely anything left, and sometimes the cupboard was bare before the end of the winter; whatever was eatable had been eaten by the tune spring came on, and most often father and son knew what it was like to go hungry. Whenever the weather was fit, they put off in their boat but often rowed back empty-handed or with one skinny flat-fish in the bottom. This did not affect their outlook. They never complained; they bore their burden of distress, heavy as it was, with the same even temper as they showed in the face of good fortune on the rare occasions it smiled on them; in this, as in everything else, they were in harmony. For them there was always comfort enough in the hope that, if they ate nothing today, God would send them a meal tomorrow—or the next day. The advancing spring found them pale and hollow- cheeked, plagued by bad dreams, so that night after night they lay awake together.—And one such spring, a spring moreover that had been colder and stormier than usual, with hardly a single day of decent weather, evil chance paid another visit to old Snjolfur's home.

Early one morning a snow-slip landed on the cabin on the Point, burying both father and son. By some inexplicable means little Snjolfur managed to scratch his way out of the drift. As soon as he realised that for all his efforts he could not dig his father out single-handed, he raced off to the village and got people out of their beds. Help came too late—the old man was suffocated when they finally reached him through the snow.

For the time being his body was laid on a flat boulder in the shelter of a shallow cave in the cliffside nearby—later they would bring a sledge to fetch him into the village. For a long time little Snjolfur stood by old Snjolfur and stroked his white hair; he murmured something as he did it, but no one heard what he said. But he did not cry and he showed no dismay. The men with the snow- shovels agreed that he was a strange lad, with not a tear for his father's death, and they were half-inclined to dislike him for it.— He's a hard one! they said, but not in admiration.—You can carry things too far.

It was perhaps because of this that no one paid any further attention to little Snjolfur. When the rescue-party and the people who had come out of mere curiosity made their way back for a bite of breakfast and a sledge for the body, the boy was left alone on the Point.

The snow-slip had shifted the cabin and it was all twisted and smashed; posts missing their laths stuck up out of the snow, tools and household gear were visible here and there—when he laid hold of them, they were as if bonded the snow. Snjolfur wandered down to the shore with the idea of seeing what had become of the boat. When he saw with what cold glee the waves were playing with its shattered fragments amongst the lumpy masses of snow below highwatermark, his frown deepened, but he did not say anything.

He did not stay long on the shore this time. When he got back to the cave, he sat down wearily on the rock beside his dead father. It's a poor look-out, he thought; he might have sold the boat if it hadn't been smashed—somewhere he had to get enough to pay for the funeral. Snjolfur had always said it was essential to have enough to cover your own funeral—there was no greater or more irredeemable disgrace than to be slipped into the ground at the expense of the parish. Fortunately his prospects weren't so bad, he had said. They could both die peacefully whenever the time came—there was the cabin, the boat, the tools and other gear, and finally the land itself—these would surely fetch enough to meet the cost of coffin and funeral service, as well as a cup of coffee for anyone who would put himself out so far as to accept their hospitality on that occasion. But now, contrary to custom, his father had not proved an oracle—he was dead and everything else had gone with him—except the land on the Point. And how was that to be turned into cash when there was no cabin on it? He would probably have to starve to death himself. Wouldn't it be simplest to run down to the shore and throw himself in the sea? But—then both he and his father would have to be buried by the parish. There were only his shoulders to carry the burden. If they both rested in a shameful grave, it would be his fault—he hadn't the heart to do it.

Little Snjolfur's head hurt with all this hard thinking. He felt he wanted to give up and let things slide. But how can a man give up when he has nowhere to live? It would be cold spending the night out here in the open.

The boy thought this out. Then he began to drag posts, pieces of rafter and other wreckage over to the cave. He laid the longest pieces sloping against the cave-mouth—he badly wanted his father to be within four walls,—covered them over and filled the gaps with bits of sail-cloth and anything else handy, and finished by shovelling snow up over the whole structure. Before long it was rather better in the cave than out-of-doors, though the most important thing was to have Snjolfur with him for his last days above ground—it might be a week or more. It was no easy matter to make a coffin and dig out frozen ground. It would certainly be a poor coffin if he had to make it himself.

When little Snjolfur had finished making his shelter, he crept inside and sat down with outstretched legs close to his father. By this time the boy was tired out and sleepy. He was on the point of dropping off, when he remembered that he had still not decided how to pay for the funeral. He was wide awake again at once. That problem had to be solved without more ado—and suddenly he saw a gleam of hope—is wasn't so unattainable after all—he might meet the cost of the funeral and maintain himself into the bargain, at any rate for a start. His drowsiness fell from him, he slipped out of the cave and strode off towards the village.

He went straight along the street in the direction of the store, looking neither to right nor left, heedless of the unfriendly glances of the villagers.—Wretched boy—he didn't even cry when his father died! were the words of those respectable, generous-hearted and high-minded folk.

When little Snjolfur got to the factor's house, he went straight into the store and asked if he might speak to the master. The storeman stared and lingered before finally shuffling to the door of the office and knocking. In a moment the door was half opened by the factor himself, who, when he caught sight of little Snjolfur and heard that he wanted to speak to him, turned to him again and, after looking him up and down, invited him in.

Little Snjolfur put his cap on the counter and did not wait to be asked twice.

Well, young man? said the factor.

The youngster nearly lost heart completely, but he screwed himself up and inquired diffidently whether the factor knew that there were unusually good landing-facilities out on the Point.

It is much worse in your landing-place than it is in ours out there.

The factor had to smile at the gravity and spirit of the boy—he confessed that he had heard it spoken of.

Then little Snjolfur came to the heart of the—if he let out the use of the landing-place on the Point to the factor for the coming summer—how much would he be willing to pay to have his Faroese crews land their catches there?—Only for the coming summer, mind!

Wouldn't it be more straightforward if I bought the Point from you? asked the factor, doing his best to conceal his amusement.

Little Snjolfur stoutly rejected this suggestion—he didn't want that.—Then I have no home—if I sell the Point, I mean.

The factor tried to get him to see that he could not live there in any case, by himself, destitute, in the open.

They will not allow it, my boy.

The lad steadfastly refused to accept the notion that he would be in the open out there—he had already built himself a shelter where he could lie snug.

And as soon as spring comes, I shall build another cabin—it needn't be big and there's a good bit of wood out there. But, as I expect you know, I've lost Snjolfur—and the boat. I don't think there's any hope of putting the bits of her together again. Now that I've no boat, I thought I might let out the landing-place, if I could make something out of it. The Faroese would be sure to give me something for the pot if I gave them a hand with launching and unloading. They could row most ways from there—I'm not exaggerating—they had to stay at home time and time again last summer, when it was easy for Snjolfur and me to put off. There's a world of difference between a deep-water landing-place and a shallow-water one—that's what Snjolfur said many a time.

The factor asked his visitor what price he had thought of putting on it for the summer. I don't know what the funeral will cost yet, replied the orphan in worried tones. At any rate I should need enough to pay for Snjolfur's funeral. Then I should count myself lucky.

Then let's say that, struck in the factor, and went on to say that he would see about the coffin and everything—there was no need for little Snjolfur to fret about it any more. Without thinking, he found himself opening the door for his guest, diminutive though he was,—but the boy stood there as if he had not seen him do it, and it was written clear on his face that he had not yet finished the business that brought him; the anxious look was still strong on his ruddy face, firm-featured beyond his years.

When are you expecting the ship with your stores?

The factor replied that it would hardly come tomorrow, perhaps the day after. It was a puzzle to know why the boy had asked—the pair of them, father and son, did not usually ask about his stores until they brought the cash to buy them.

Little Snjolfur did not take his eyes from the factor's face. The words stuck in his throat, but at last he managed to get his question out: In that case, wouldn't the factor be needing a boy to help in the store?

The factor did not deny it.

But he ought to be past his confirmation for preference, he added with a smile.

It looked as if little Snjolfur was ready for this answer, and indeed his errand was now at an end, but he asked the factor to come out with him round the corner of the store. They went out, the boy in front, and onto the pebble-bank nearby. The boy stopped at a stone lying there, got a grip of it, lifted it without any obvious exertion and heaved it away from him. Then he turned to the factor.

We call this stone the Weakling. The boy you had last summer couldn't lift it high enough to let the damp in underneath—much less any further!

Oh, well then, seeing you are stronger than he was, it ought to be possible to make use of you in some way, even though you are on the wrong side of confirmation, replied the factor in a milder tone.

Do I get my keep while I'm with you? And the same wages as he had? continued the youngster, who was the sort that likes to know where he stands in good time.

But of course, answered the factor, who for once was in no mood to drive a hard bargain.

That's good—then I shan't go on the parish, said little Snjolfur, and was easier in his mind. The man who has got something to pot in himself and on himself isn't a pauper,—Snjolfur often used to say that, he added, and he straightened himself up proudly and offered his hand to the factor, just as he had seen his father do. Good-bye, he said. I shall come then—not tomorrow but the day after.

The factor told him to come in again for a minute and leading the way to the kitchen-door he ushered little Snjolfur into the warmth. He asked the cook if she couldn't give this nipper here a bite of something to eat, preferably something warm—he could do with it.

Little Snjolfur would not accept any food.

Aren't you hungry? asked the astonished factor.

The boy could not deny that he was—and for the rest he could hardly get his words out with the sharpness of his hunger whetted still keener by the blessed smell of cooking. But he resisted the temptation:

I am not a beggar, he said.

The factor was upset and he saw that he had set about it clumsily. He went over to the dogged youngster, patted his head and, with a nod to the cook, led little Snjolfur into the dining-room.

Have you never seen your father give his visitors a drink or offer them a cup of coffee when they came to see him? he asked, and he gave his words a resentful tone.

Little Snjolfur had to confess that his father had sometimes offered hospitality to a visitor.

There you are then, said the factor. It's just ordinary good manners to offer hospitality—and to accept it. Refusing a well-meant invitation for no reason can mean the end of a friendship. You are a visitor here, so naturally I offer you something to eat: we have made an important deal and, what's more, we have come to terms over a job. If you won't accept ordinary hospitality, it's hard to see how the rest is going to work out.

The boy sighed: of course, it must be as the factor said. But he was in a hurry. Snjolfur was by himself out on the Point. His eyes wandered round the room—then he added, very seriously: The point is to pay your debts, not owe anybody anything, and trust in Providence.

There was never a truer word spoken, agreed the factor, and as he said it he pulled his handkerchief out of his pocket. He's a chip of the old block, he muttered, and putting his hand on little Snjolfur's shoulder, he blessed him.

The boy was astonished to see a grown man with tears in his eyes.

Snjolfur never cried, he said, and went on: I haven't cried either since I was little—I nearly did when I knew Snjolfur was dead. But I was afraid he wouldn't like it, and I stopped myself.

A moment later and tears overwhelmed little Snjolfur.—It is a consolation, albeit a poor one, to lean for a while on the bosom of a companion.

GUDMUNDUR G. HAGALIN

THE FOX SKIN

No need to take care now about fastening the door, Arni of Bali said to himself as he wrapped the string around the nail driven into the door-post of the outlying sheepcote. Then he turned around, took out his handkerchief, and, putting it to his nose, blew vigorously. This done, he folded the handkerchief together again, wiped his mouth and nose, and took out his snuff horn.

What fine balmy weather, thought Arni. That miserable fox won't come near sheepcotes or houses now. Blast its hide! Yes, it had caused him many a wakeful night. All the neighbouring farmers would have the fool's luck to catch a fox every single winter. All but him. He couldn't even wound a vixen, and had in all his life never caught any kind of fox. Wouldn't it be fun to bring home a dark brown pelt, one with fine overhair? Yes, wouldn't that be fun? Arni shook his head in delight, cleared his throat vigorously, and took a pinch of snuff.

Bending his steps homeward, he tottered along with his body half stooped, as was his habit, and his hands behind his back. When he looked up, he did not straighten out, but bent his neck back so his head lay between his shoulder blades. Then his red-rimmed eyes looked as if they were about to pop out of his head, his dark red beard rose up as though striving to free itself from its roots, and his empurpled nose and scarlet cheek-bones protruded.

Pretty good under foot, thought Arni. At least it was easy to go between the sheepcotes and the house. Everything pretty quiet just now. The sheep took care of themselves during the day, and grazing was plentiful along the seashore and on the hillsides. No reason why he might not now and then lie in wait somewhat into the night in the hope of catching a fox; he wasn't too tired for that. But he had given up all that sort of thing. It brought only vexation and trouble. Besides, he had told everybody that he did not think it worth his while to waste his time on such things and perhaps catch his death to boot. The Lord knew that was mere pretence. Eighty crowns for a beautiful, dark brown fox skin was a tidy sum! But a man had to think up something to say for himself, the way they all harped on fox-hunting: Bjarni of Fell caught a white vixen night before last, or Einar of Brekka caught a brown dog-fox yesterday. Or if a man stepped over to a neighbour's for a moment: Any hunting? Anyone shot a fox? Our Gisli here caught a grayish brown one last evening. Such incessant twaddle!

Arni's breath came short. Wasn't it enough if a man made an honest living? Yet, work or achievement which brought no joy was unblessed. At this point Samur darted up. Arni thought the dog had deserted him and rushed off home. Now, what in the world ailed the creature? Shame on you for a pesky cur! Can't you be still a minute, you brute? Must I beat you? asked Arni, making threatening gestures at Samur, a large, black-spotted dog with ugly, shaggy hair. But Samur darted away, ran off whimpering; he would pause now and then and look back at his master, until finally he disappeared behind a big boulder.

What's got into the beast? He can't have found a fox trail, can he?

Arni walked straight to the rock where Samur had disappeared; then slowing down his pace, he tiptoed as if he expected to find a fox hidden there. Yes, there was Samur. There he lay in front of a hole, whimpering and wagging his tail.

Shame on you, Samur!

Arni lay down prone on the snow and stretched his arm into the hole. But all of a sudden he jerked his hand back, his heart beating as if it would tear itself out of his breast. He had so plainly felt something furry inside the hole, and he was badly mistaken if a strong fox odour did not come out of it. Was the fox alive, or was it dead? Might it bite him fatally? But that made no difference. Now that he had a good chance of taking a fox, it was do or die. He stood up straight and stretched every muscle, and pulled the mitten on his right hand carefully up over his wrist. Then he knelt down, thrust his hand in the hole, set his teeth, and screwed up his face. Yes, now he had caught hold of it and was pulling it carefully out. Well, well, well, well! Not so bad! A dark brown tail, a glossy body, and what fine over-hair! For once Arni of Bali had some luck! The fox was dead; it had been shot in the belly and just crept in there to die. Sly devil! Poor beast! Blessed creature! Arni ended by feeling quite tenderly towards the fox. He hardly knew how to give utterance to his joy.

Good old Samur, my own precious dog, let me pat you, said Arni, rubbing the dog's cheek with his own. They could shout themselves blue in the face. It was no trick to kill all you wanted of these little devils if you just had the powder and shot and were willing to waste your time on it. But here Arni's face fell. He did not even have his gun with him. It stood, all covered with rust, at home out in the shed. Just his luck! And how could he claim to have shot a fox without a gun?—Get out of here, Samur. Shame on you, you rascal!—And Arni booted Samur so hard that the dog yelped.

But, in direst need, help is at hand. He could wait for the cover of darkness. Not even his wife should know but that he had shot the fox. Wouldn't she stare at him? She had always defied him and tried to belittle him. No, she should not learn the truth, she least of all. He would not tell a soul. Now Samur, he knew how to hold his tongue, faithful creature! Arni sat down on the rock, with the fox on his knees, and started singing to pass the time, allowing his good cheer to ring out as far as his voice would carry:

My fine Sunday cap has been carried away
By a furious gale;
And I'll wear it no more to the chapel to pray
In the wind and the hail.

He chanted this ballad over and over again until he was tired, then sat still, smiling and stroking the fox skin. He had learned the song when he was a child from his mother, who had sung it all day long one spring while she was shearing the sheep. And he could not think of any other for the moment. It wasn't, in fact, a bad song. There were many good rhymesters in Iceland. He began singing again, rocking his body back and forth vehemently, and stroking the fox skin the while. And Samur, who sat in front of him, cocked his head first on one side, then on the other, and gave him a knowing look. At last the dog stretched out his neck, raised his muzzle into the air and howled, using every variation of key known to him. At this Arni stopped short and stared at him, then bending his head slightly to one side to study him, he roared with laughter.

What an extraordinary dog! Yes, really extraordinary.

In the little kitchen at Bali, Groa, the mistress, crouched before the stove and poked the fire with such vigour that both ashes and embers flew out on the floor. She was preparing to heat a mouthful of porridge for supper for her old man and the brats. She stood up, rubbed her eyes and swore. The horrid smoke that always came from that rattletrap of a stove! And that wretched old fool of a husband was not man enough to fix it! Oh, no, he wasn't handy enough for that; he went at every blessed thing as if his fingers were all thumbs. And where could he be loafing tonight? Not home yet! Serve him right if she locked the house and allowed him to stay in the sheepcotes, or wherever it was he was dawdling. There now, those infernal brats were at the spinning wheel. Groa jumped up, darted into the passage, and went to the stairs.

Will you leave that spinning wheel be, you young devils? If you break the flier or the upright, your little old mother will be after you.

A dead calm ensued. So Groa returned to the kitchen, and taking a loaf of pot-bread from the cupboard, cut a few slices and spread them with dripping.

Now a scratching sound was heard at the door, and Arni entered.

Good evening to all, said he with urbanity, as he set down the gun behind the kitchen door. Here's that gun. It has certainly paid for itself, poor old thing.

His wife did not reply to his greeting, but she eyed him askance with a look that was anything but loving.

Been fooling around with that gun! Why the blazes couldn't you have come home and brought me a bit of peat from the pit? A fine hunter you are! I might as well have married the devil.—And his wife turned from him with a sneer.

You're in a nice temper now, my dear. But just take a look at this, said Arni, throwing down the brown fox on the kitchen floor.

At first Groa stared at her husband as if she had never seen him before. Then she shook her head and smiled sarcastically.

You found it dead, I'll wager!

Arni started. His face turned red and his eyes protruded.

You would say that! You don't let me forget what a superior woman I married! Found it dead!—And Arni plumped down on the woodbox.

His wife laughed.

I'll wager I hit the nail on the head that time!

Arni jumped to his feet. That confounded old witch should not spoil his pleasure.

You're as stark, raving mad as you always have been. But I don't care what you say. Kids, come and look at the fox your father has shot.

Three days later they had a visitor. Arni stood outside and stared at him. For a wonder, somebody had at last found his way to Arni's. Days and nights had passed, but nobody had come. They always came when they weren't wanted. And now came Jon of Lon, that overbearing fellow! But now he could see that Arni of Bali was also a man among men.

> Howdy, Arni, you poor fish! said Jon, fixing his steely gray eyes on Arni.
>
> How are you, you old snake! answered Arni, smiling contemptuously.

> What monstrous eyes Jon had when he looked at a
> person!

Has something special happened? You're somehow so puffed up today, said Jon with a sarcastic smile.

Darn him! muttered Arni. Was he going to act just like Groa? In that case, Arni had at least a trump card in reserve.

Did you say something? inquired Jon, sticking a quid of tobacco into his mouth. Or wasn't it meant for my ears? Oh, well, I don't care for your mutterings, you poor wretch. But now, go ask your wife to give me a little drink of sour whey.

Arni turned round slowly and lazily. Wasn't the old fellow going to notice the skin? It wasn't so small that it couldn't be seen. There it hung on the wall, right in the sunlight, combed and beautifully glossy.

That's quite a nice fox skin. Whose is it? asked Jon, walking over to the wall.

Arni turned round. He could feel his heart beating fast.

Mine, he said, with what calm he could muster.

What is the idea of you buying a fox skin, you poor beggar?

Buying? Arni sighed. You think I can't shoot me a fox?

You! Jon laughed. That's a downright lie, my dear Arni.

A lie! You'd best not tell people they lie unless you know more about it. A scoundrel like you, I say, a scoundrel like you! replied Arni, swelling. I think you'd better be getting in and see her. You know her pretty well, I believe.

Jon looked at the farmer of Bali with his steely eyes.

For whom are you keeping the skin, Arni?

No one, said Arni, crossly; then after some hesitation: The Lord gave it to me.

All right, Arni. Miracles never cease. That is plain enough after this, and no question about it. That's an eighty-crown skin, however you came by it. But now let's go in and see Groa. As you say, I know her pretty well. She was a smart girl, you poor wretch. Too bad I was married and had to throw her to a creature like you.

Arni grinned and, trotting to the door of the house, called: Groa, a visitor to see you.

The woman came to the door. A smile played about her lips, smouldering embers glowed in her blue eyes, and the sunlight lighted up the unkempt braids of golden hair which fell down about her pale cheeks.

But Arni for once was satisfied. At last Jon was properly impressed. The affair between Groa and Jon was something that could not be helped. Jon surely regretted having lost that girl! Yes, indeed! And she had her good points. She was smart, and a hundred crowns a year, besides everything else that was brought them from Lon, was pretty good compensation. Yes, many a man had married less well than Arni of Bali. And the children were his, most of them, anyway. Nobody need tell him anything else.

The fox skin became Arni of Bali's most cherished possession. Every day, when the weather was clear, he would hang it, well smoothed and combed, on the outside wall, and when he left home he carefully put it away in a safe place. The skin became famous throughout the district, and many of the younger men made special trips to Bali to examine it. Arni would beam with joy and strut around with a knowing, self-satisfied expression on his face, and would tell of the patience, the agility, and the marksmanship he had to put into killing this monstrously clever fox. It certainly wasn't hard to kill all you wanted of these devils, if you just had the powder and shot and were willing to give your time to it, he would say, as he turned the skin so that the sunlight shone full on the glossy pelt.

Then one day that fall, Arni came home from tending the sheep, which had just been brought down from the mountain pastures. He hung the skin out and went into the kitchen, where Groa was busy washing, sat down on a box by the wall on the other side of the room, let his head rest on his hands, and looked wise. For a while there was silence. At last Groa looked up from her washtub and gave Arni a piercing glance.

Have you got your eye on a cow to replace the greyspotted one we killed last spring?

Cow? asked Arni, scratching his head. Cow? Yes, so you say, my good woman.

So I say? Do you think the milk from Dumba alone goes very far in feeding such a flock of children as we have? You haven't gone and squandered the money we got for Skjalda? asked Groa, looking harder still at her husband.

Don't be foolish, woman! The money lies untouched at the factor's. But he wouldn't pay much for the meat and hide of Skjalda, not anywhere near enough to buy a good milking cow. He said the English on the trawlers don't set much store by cow's meat. The summer has been only so-so, and I'm sure we'll have plenty of uses for what money I've been able to scrape together. Of course, a cow is a good thing to buy, an enjoyable luxury, if only you have plenty of money.

If you can't scrape together the money for a cow, we must cut expenses somehow. Perhaps you could stop stuffing your nostrils with that dirty snuff? And you ought at any rate to be able to sell that fancy fox skin you play with so childishly.

Is that so!

Yes, you play with that wretched fox skin just exactly like any crazy youngster.

Wretched is it? Take care what you say, woman! Wretched skin! A fine judge of such matters you are!—And standing up, Arni paced the kitchen floor.—An eighty-crown skin! And you call it wretched! Jon of Lon didn't call it any names. You'll believe at least what he says.

Now, don't get puffed up. You ought to be thankful to get what you can for the skin. It will help in buying the cow.

The cow? Let me tell you, woman, that I am not going to buy a cow for the skin. You can take it from me that you will never get a cow for that skin. Or anything else, in fact. The farmer at Lon can shell out whatever is needed for buying the cow. That's the least he can do for you.

Groa stopped her washing, stared for a few seconds at Arni, and then with a quick movement walked up to him, brandishing a bit of wet linen.

Will you tell me what you're going to do with the skin? she asked, almost in a whisper.

Arni shrank back. The way to the door was cut off. He raised his arm in self-defence and retreated as far as possible into the corner.

I'm going to sell it. Now be reasonable, Groa. I'm going to sell it.

And what are you going to buy for it? his wife hissed, boring into him with her eyes.

A cow. I'm going to buy a cow for it.

You lie! You know you're not going to sell it. You're going to play with it. Know your children hungering for milk and play with the skin!

My children?

No, God be praised, they're—not—yours, said Groa, allowing the blows to rain on Arni.—But now I'll keep the skin for you.—And like an arrow she shot out of the door, all out of breath and trembling.

For a few seconds Arni stood still. His eyes seemed bursting out of their sockets, and the hair in his beard stood on end. In a flash he rushed over the kitchen floor and out of the house.

Groa had just taken the skin down off the nail on the wall. Now she brandished it and looked at Arni with fury in her gaze. But he did not wait. He rushed at her, gave her such a shove that she fell, and, snatching the skin from her, ran. A safe distance away, he turned and stood panting for several seconds. At last, exhausted and trembling with rage, he hissed:

I tell you, Groa. I'll have my way about this. The skin is the only thing that is all my own, and no one shall take it from me.

Arni fled then. He took to his heels, and ran away as fast as he could up the slopes.

Far in the innermost corner of the outlying sheepcote at Bali, to which the sun's rays never reach, Arni built himself a little cupboard. This cupboard is kept carefully locked, and Arni carries the key on a string which hangs around his neck. Arni now has become quite prosperous. For a long time it was thought that he must keep money in the cupboard, but last spring an acquaintance of his stopped at the outlying sheepcote on his way from the village. The man had some liquor with him and gave Arni a taste. At last the visitor was allowed to see what the cupboard contained—a carefully combed and smoothed dark brown fox skin. Arni was visibly moved by the unveiling of his secret. Staring at the ceiling, he licked his whiskers and sighed deeply.

It seems to me, Gisli, he said to his friend, that I'd rather lose all my ewes than this skin, for it was the thing which once made me say, 'Thus far and no farther!' And since then I seem to own something right here in my breast which not even Jon of Lon can take away from me. I think I am now beginning to understand what is meant in the Scriptures by 'the treasure which neither moth nor rust can currupt.'

Arni's red-rimmed eyes were moist. For a while he stood there thinking. But all of a sudden he shook his head and, turning to his acquaintance, said: Let's see the bottle. A man seems to feel warmer inside if he gets a little drop.—And Arni shook himself as if the mental strain of his philosophizing had occasioned in him a slight chill.

HALLDOR KILJAN LAXNESS

NEW ICELAND

The road leads from Old Iceland to New Iceland. It is the way of men from the old to the new in the hope that the new will be better than the old. So Torfi Torfason has sold his sheep and his cows and his horses, torn himself away from his land, and journeyed to America— where the raisins grow all over the place and where a much brighter future awaits us and our children. And he took his ewes by the horn for the last time, led them to the highest bidder, and said: Now this one is my good Goldbrow who brings back her two lambs from Mulata every fall. And what do you say to the coat of wool on Bobbin here? She's a fine sturdy lass, Bobbin, isn't she?

And thus he sold them one after another, holding them himself by the horn. And he pressed their horns against the callouses on his palm for the last time. These were his ewes, who had crowded around the manger in the dead of winter and stuck their noses into the fragrant hay. And when he came home from the long trip to the market town after having wrangled with some of the rascals there, he marvelled at how snow-white they were in the fleece. They were like a special kind of people and yet better than people in general. And yonder were his cows being led off the place like large and foolish women, who are nevertheless kindness itself, and you are fond of them because you have known them since you were young. They were led out through the lanes, and strange boys urged them on with bits of strap. And he patted his horses on the rump for the last time and sold them to the highest bidder, these fine old fellows who were perhaps the only beings in the world that understood him and knew him and esteemed him. He had known them since they were boys full of pomp and show. Now he sold them for money because the way of man leads from the old to the new, from Old Iceland to New Iceland, and, the evening after this sale, he no more thought of saying his prayers than would a man who had taken God Almighty by the horn, patted Him on the rump, and sold Him, and let some strange boy urge Him on with a bit of strap. He felt that he was an evil man, a downright ungodly man, and he asked his wife what the devil she was sniffling about.

In the middle of July a new settler put up a log cabin on a grassy plot in the swamps along Icelandic River, a short distance from what is now called Riverton in New Iceland. Torfi hung the picture of Jon Sigurdsson on one wall, and on another his wife hung a calendar with a picture of a girl in a wide-brimmed hat. The neighbours were helpful to them in building their cabin, making ditches, and in other ways. All that summer Torfi stood up to his hips in mud digging ditches, and when the bottom was worn out of his shoes and the soles of his feet began to get sore from the shovel, he hit on a plan: he cut the bottom out of a tin can and stuck his toe into the cylinder. And the first evening when he came home from the ditch- digging. and was struggling to remove from himself that sticky clay which is peculiar to the soil of Manitoba, he could not help saying to his wife: It's really remarkable how filthy the mud is here in New Iceland.

But that summer there was an epidemic among the children, and Torfi Torfason lost two of his four, a six-year old girl and a three-year old boy. Their names were Jon and Maria. The neighbours helped him to make a coffin. A clergyman was brought from a distance, and he buried Jon and Maria, and Torfi Torfason paid what was asked. A few not very well washed Icelanders, their old hats in their toil-worn hands, stood over the grave and droned sadly. Torfi Torfason had seen to it that every body would get coffee and fritters and Christmas cakes. But when autumn came, the weather grew cold and the snow fell, and then his wife had a new baby who filled the log cabin with fresh crying. This was a Canadian Icelander. After that came Indian Summer with the multi-coloured forests.

And the Indians came down from the North by their winding trails along the river and wanted to buy themselves mittens. They took things very calmly and did not fuss about trifles, but bought a single pair of mittens for a whole haunch of venison together with the shoulder. Then they bought a scarf and socks for a whole carcass. After that they trudged off again with their mittens and scarfs like any other improvident wretches.

Then came the winter, and what was to be done now? Torfi christened his farm Riverbank. There was only one cow at Riverbank, three children, and very little in the cupboard. The cow's name was Mulley, in spite of the fact that she had very long horns, and she was known as Riverbank

Mulley. And she had big eyes and stared like a foreigner at the farmer's wife and mooed every time anybody walked past the door.

I don't think poor Mulley will be able to feed us all this winter, said Torfi Torfason.

Have you thought of anything? asked Torfi Torfason's wife.

Nothing unless to go north and fish in the lake. It's said that those who go there often do well for themselves.

I was thinking that if you went somewhere, I might just as well go somewhere too for the winter. Sigridur of New Farm says there's lots of work for washerwomen in Winnipeg in the winter. Some of the women from this district are going south the beginning of next week. I could pack up my old clothes on a sled like them and go too. I'd just leave little Tota here with the youngsters. She's going on fourteen now, Tota is.

I could perhaps manage to send home a mess of fish once in a while, said Torfi Torfason.

This was an evening early in November, snow had fallen on the woods, the swamps were frozen over. They spoke no more of their parting. Jon Sigurdsson grinned out into the room, and the calendar girl with the wide-brimmed hat laid her blessing upon the sleeping children.

The tiny kerosene lamp burned in the window, but the frost flowers bloomed on the window-panes.

> It seems to me it can get cold here, no less than at home,
> said Torfi Torfason presently.

Do you remember what fun it often was when guests came in the evening? There would be sure to be talk about the sheep at this time of the autumn on our farm.

Oh, it's not much of a sheep country here in the west, said Torfi Torfason. But there's fishing in the lake ... And if you have decided to go south and get yourself a 'job', as they say here, then ...

If you write to Iceland, be sure to ask about our old cow Skjalda, how she is getting along. Our old Skjalda. Good old cow.

Silence.

Then Torfi Torfason's wife spoke again:

By the way, what do you think of the cows here in America, Torfi? Don't you think they're awfully poor milkers? Somehow or other I feel as if I could never get fond of Mulley. It seems to me as if it would be impossible to let yourself get fond of a foreign cow.

Oh, that's just a notion, said Torfi Torfason, spitting through his teeth, although he had long since given up chewing. Why shouldn't the cows here be up and down just the same as other cows? But there's one thing sure. I'll never get so attached to another horse again, since I sold my Skjoni ... There was a fine fellow.

They never referred in any other way than this to what they had owned or what they had lost, but sat long silent, and the tiny lamp cast a glow on the frost flowers like a garden—two poor Icelanders, man and wife, who put out their light and go to sleep. Then begins the great, soundless, Canadian winter night.—

The women started off for Winnipeg a few days later, walking through the snow-white woods, over the frozen fields, a good three days' journey. They tied their belongings on to sleds. Each one drew her own sled. This was known as going washing in Winnipeg. Torfi Torfason remained at home one night longer.

He stood in the front yard outside of the cabin and looked after the women as they disappeared into the woods with their sleds. The November forests listened in the frost to the speech of these foreign women, echoed it, without understanding it. Ahead of them, walked an old man to lead the way. They wore Icelandic homespun skirts, and had them tucked up at the waist. Around their heads, they had tied Icelandic woollen shawls. They say they are such good walkers. They intend to take lodging somewhere for the night for their pennies.

When the women had disappeared, Torfi Torfason looked into the cabin where they had drunk their last drop of coffee, and the mugs were still standing unwashed on the ledge. Tota was taking care of the little boy, but little Imba was sitting silent beside the stove. Mamma had gone away. Torfi Torfason patched up the door, patched up the walls, all that day, and carried in wood. In the evening, the little girls bring him porridge, bread, and a slice of meat. The little boy frets and cries. And his sister, big Tota with her big red hands, takes him up in her arms and rocks him: Little brother must be good, little brother mustn't cry, little brother's going to get a drop of milk from his good old Mulley.—But the boy keeps on crying.

> My Mulley cow, moo, moo, moo
> Mulley in the byre,

What great big horns she has.
What great big eyes she has!
Blessings on my Mulley cow, my good old
Mulley cow.

Our Mamma went away, 'way, 'way,
Away went our Mamma.
Our Mamma's gone but where, where, where.
Where has she gone, our Mamma?
She'll come back after Christmas and
Christmas and Christmas,
Back with a new dress for me, a new dress,
a new dress.

We mustn't be a-crying, a-crying, a-crying,
For surely she'll be coming, our Mamma,
our Mamma,

For she is our good Mamma, our Mamma,
our Mamma.
God bless our Mamma and our little brother's
Mamma.

But the boy still kept on crying. And Torfi Torfason ate his meal like a man who is trying to eat something in a hurry at a concert.

The day after, Torfi Torfason started off. A Canadian winter day, blue, vast, and calm, with ravens hovering over the snow-covered woods. He threaded his way along the trails northward to the lake, carrying his pack on his back. This was through unsettled country, nowhere a soul, nowhere the smoke from a cabin mile after mile, only those ravens, flying above the white woods and alighting on the branches as on a clay statue of Pallas. 'Nevermore.' And Torfi Torfason thinks of his ewes and his cows and his horses and all that he has lost.

Then all of a sudden a wretched bitch waddled out from the woods into his path. It was a vagrant bitch, as thin as a skeleton, and so big in the belly that she walked with difficulty. Her dugs dragged along the snow, for she was in pup. They came from opposite directions, two lonely creatures, who are paddling their own canoes in America, and meet one cold winter day out in the snow. At first she pricked up her ears and stared at the man with brown mistrustful eyes. Then she crouched down in the snow and began to tremble, and he understood that she was telling him she wasn't feeling well, that she had lost her master, that she had often been beaten, beaten, beaten, and never in her life had enough to eat, and that nobody had ever been kind to her, never; nobody knew, she was sure, how all this would end for her. She was very poor, she said.

Well, it takes all kinds to make a world, said Torfi Torfason. And he took off his pack and sat down in the snow with his legs stretched out in front of him. In the mouth of the pack there was something that little Tota had scraped together for her papa on the trip. And then the bitch began to wag her tail back and forth in the snow and gaze with lustful eyes at the mouth of the pack.

Well, well, poor doggie, so you have lost your master and have had nothing to eat since God knows when, and I've just chased out my wife, yes, yes, and she went away yesterday. Yes, yes, she's going to try to shift for herself as a washerwoman down in Winnipeg this winter, yes, yes, that's how it is now. Yes, yes, we packed up and left a fairly decent living there at home and came here into this damnable log-cabin existence, yes, yes. ... Well, try that in your chops, you miserable cur, you can gobble that up, I tell you. Oh, this is nothing but damned scraps and hardly fit to offer a dog, not even a stray dog, oh, no. Well, I can't bring myself to chase you away, poor wretch—we're all stray dogs in the eyes of the Lord in any case, that's what we all are....

Time passed on and Torfi Torfason fished in the lake and lived in a hut on some outlying island with his boss, a red-bearded man, who made money out of his fishing fleet as well as by selling other fishermen tobacco, liquor, and twine. The fisherman vehemently disliked the dog and said every day that that damned bitch ought to be killed. He had built this cabin on the island himself. It was divided into two parts, a hall and a room. They slept in the room, and in the hall they kept fishing tackle, food, and other supplies, but the bitch slept on the step outside the cabin door. The fisherman was not a generous man and gave Torfi the smaller share of the food. He absolutely forbade giving the dog the tiniest morsel and said that bitch ought to be killed. To this Torfi made no answer, but always stole a bite for the dog when the fisherman had gone to bed. Now the time came when the bitch was to pup. The bitch pupped. And when she had finished pupping, he gave her a fine chunk of meat, which he stole from the fisherman, for he knew that bitter is the hunger of the woman in child-bed, and let her lie on an old sack in the hall, directly against the will of the fisherman. Then he lay down to sleep.

But he had not lain long when he is aroused by someone walking about and he cannot figure out why. But it turns out to be the fisherman, who gets up out of bed, walks out into the hall. lights the lamp, takes the bitch by the scruff of the neck, and throws her out in the snow. Then he closes the outer door, puts out the light, and lies down on his bunk. Now it is quiet for a while, until the bitch begins to howl outside and the pups to whine piteously in the hall. Then Torfi Torfason gets up, gropes his way out through the hall, lets the bitch in, and she crawls at once over her pups. After that he lies down to sleep. But he has not lain long when he is aroused by somebody walking about and he can not figure out why. But it turns out to be the fisherman, who gets up out of bed, walks out into the hall, lights the lamp, takes the bitch by the scruff of her neck for the second time and throws her out into the snow. Then he lies down to sleep again. Again the bitch begins to howl outside and the pups to whine, and Torfi Torfason gets up out of bed, lets the bitch in to the pups again, and again lies down. After a little while the fisherman gets up again, lights the lantern, and fares forth. But even soft iron can be whetted sharp, and now Torfi Torfason springs out of bed a third time and out into the hall after the fisherman.

Either you leave the dog alone or both of us will go, I and the dog, says Torfi Torfason, and it was only a matter of seconds till he laid hands on his master. A hard scuffle began and the cabin shook with it, and everything fell over and broke that was in the way. They gave each other many and heavy blows, but the fisherman was the more warlike, until Torfi tackled low, grasped him round the waist, and did not let up in the attack until he had the fisherman doubled up with his chin against his knees. Then he opened the door of the cabin and threw him out somewhere into the wide world.

Outside, the weather was calm, the stars were shining, it was extremely cold, and there was snow over everything. Torfi was all black and blue and bleeding, hot and panting after the struggle. So this was what had to happen to Torfi Torfason, renowned as a man of peace, who had never harmed a living creature—to throw a man out of his own house, hurl him out on the frozen ground in the middle of the night, and all for one she-dog. Perhaps I have even killed him, Torfi thought, but that's the end of that—that's how it had to be. To think that I ever moved to New Iceland!

And he sauntered out of the cabin, coatless as he stood, sauntered out on to the icy ground and headed for the woods. And he had hardly walked twenty feet when he had forgotten both his rage and the fisherman and started to think about what he had owned and what he had lost. Nobody knows what he has owned until he has lost it. He began to think about his sheep, which were as white as snow in the fleece, about his horses, fine old fellows, who were the only ones who understood him and knew him and esteemed him, and about his cows, which were led out the lanes one evening last spring and strange boys ran after them with bits of strap. And he began to think about Jon and Maria, whom God Almighty had taken to Himself up in yon great, foreign heaven, which vaults over New Iceland and is something altogether different from the heaven at home. And he saw still in his mind those Icelandic pioneers who had stood over the grave with their old hats in their sorely tired hands and droned.

And he threw himself down on the frozen ground among the trees and cried bitterly in the frosty night—this big strong man who had gone all the way from Old Iceland to New Iceland—this proletarian who had brought his children as a sacrifice to the hope of a much worthier future, a more perfect life. His tears fell on the ice.